Matt broke their kiss, his breathing ragged

"I've been wanting to kiss you for so long.... Did anyone ever tell you that you kiss with as much sugar and spice as you talk?"

Paige wanted to clap her hands over her ears. How could she have allowed him to kiss her? She tried to extricate herself from his embrace.

"Matt, I can't—"

"Why not?" he interrupted her, loosening his hold around her. "You just did." He tenderly cupped her chin when she tried to back farther away from him. "And if I'm not mistaken, you enjoyed it as much as I did."

Paige colored and her eyes stung with a fresh batch of tears. Her voice rose sharply. "If you must know, I can't get involved with anyone right now—particularly nearly naked men—because I'm pregnant and I don't know who the father is!"

Dear Harlequin Intrigue Reader,

Harlequin Intrigue has just celebrated its fifteenth anniversary and we're proud to continue to bring to you thrilling romantic suspense that leaves you breathless!—plus your favorite ongoing miniseries—into the new millennium.

To start the New Year off right, Kelsey Roberts launches into the second installment of her new series, THE LANDRY BROTHERS, with *Landry's Law* (#545). Over the next year you can expect more exciting Landry stories. Don't miss any!

We're also continuing our amnesia promotion A MEMORY AWAY... This month a woman wakes up with no memory and morning sickness, but she can't remember who's the father in *The Baby Secret* (#546) by Joyce Sullivan. And if you love a good twins story you must not miss *Twice Tempted* (#547) by Harper Allen. Finally, Harlequin Intrigue newcomer C.J. Carmichael explores the life of a devoted man of the law and the woman for whom he'll break all the rules in *Same Place, Same Time* (#548).

It's romance. It's suspense. It's Harlequin Intrigue.

Enjoy, and Happy New Year!

Sincerely,

Denise O'Sullivan
Associate Senior Editor
Harlequin Intrigue

P.S. Starting next month, Harlequin Intrigue has a new look! Watch for us at your favorite retail outlet.

The Baby Secret
Joyce Sullivan

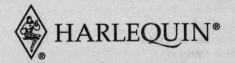

HARLEQUIN®

TORONTO • NEW YORK • LONDON
AMSTERDAM • PARIS • SYDNEY • HAMBURG
STOCKHOLM • ATHENS • TOKYO • MILAN • MADRID
PRAGUE • WARSAW • BUDAPEST • AUCKLAND

To Patrick Gilles David, who teaches me all about little boys

My sincere thanks to the following people for giving this story a sense
of realism. Any mistakes are my own.

Pat and Linda Poitevin; Corporal Darryl Little, Whistler, B.C.
RCMP; Jackie Oakley, Ottawa-Carleton Police;
Amanda Steinberg; T. Lorraine Vassalo, Criminologist;
Adrian Gregory and Liza Walli, heli-skiing experts;
Francois Tremblay, Chartered Financial Planner;
Bert and Judy McAnerin; Grace Green;
Debbie Kingdon; Dr. Stephen W. MacLean;
Danielle Ferron, Ph.D.; and Patrick David.
Special thanks to Barbara Dabrowski

ISBN 0-373-22546-6

THE BABY SECRET

Copyright © 1999 by Joyce David

Visit us at www.romance.net

Printed in U.S.A.

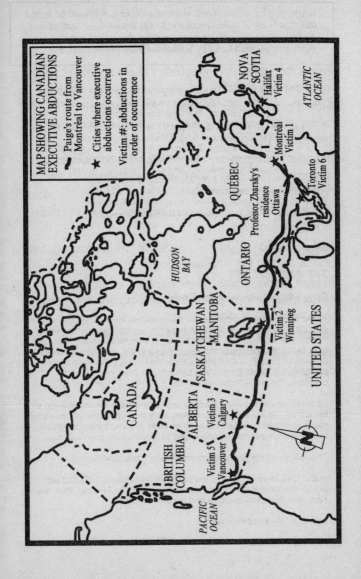

MAP SHOWING CANADIAN
EXECUTIVE ABDUCTIONS

- - - Paige's route from
Montréal to Vancouver

★ Cities where executive
abductions occurred

Victim #: abductions in
order of occurrence

ATLANTIC
OCEAN

NOVA
SCOTIA
Halifax
Victim 4

Montréal
Victim 1

Toronto
Victim 6

Professor Zbarsky's
residence
Ottawa

QUÉBEC

ONTARIO

HUDSON
BAY

CANADA

Victim 2
Winnipeg

MANITOBA

SASKATCHEWAN

ALBERTA

Victim 3
Calgary

BRITISH
COLUMBIA

Victim 5
Vancouver

UNITED STATES

PACIFIC
OCEAN

N

CAST OF CHARACTERS

Paige Roberts — Why couldn't she remember who fathered her child?

Matt Darby/Hollis Fenton — Was the woman he'd fallen in love with involved in his abduction and attempted murder?

Brenda Thompson — Her husband was abducted and murdered and Paige was trying to help her find who was responsible.

Joseph Zbarsky — This criminologist saw a pattern in the abductions.

Luther Hollis — Had his insistence on contacting the police sealed his nephew's fate?

Evelyn Hollis-Styles — Her nephew's murder gave her a chance to show the board of directors what she could really do.

Noreen Muir — Hollis's loyal secretary?

Ken Whitfield — He blamed Hollis for his daughter's death.

Prologue

He'd be dead soon.

The trunk of the car was too small and dark and suffocating. Hollis Fenton could barely breathe through the black velvet bag that covered his head. His wrists were securely bound to his ankles behind him, rendering him completely helpless. He could feel the car taking a series of curves and had the sensation they were driving up a winding hill. Into the North Shore mountains? He wasn't sure. All he knew is that they were going to kill him.

Regret that he hadn't told Paige he loved her burned in the back of his throat. He'd thought they had all the time in the world. And what man in his right mind proposed to a woman after knowing her for a week? After making love to her twice in one night?

Had she driven east to Montreal when he hadn't kept their Saturday night dinner date after their night together? Did she think he was a jerk for not calling? Hollis had no idea if his kidnapping was public knowledge. But it would soon be, he was sure.

An image of Paige as she'd walked into his office

ten days ago flashed in his mind with the magical glitter of a spun-glass Christmas ornament.

Silver and gold. Luminous silver eyes, golden glimmering hair. A face that could be a mold for angels. He'd sucked in his breath in instant reaction, wondering if she could be as honest and sincere as that fresh face implied.

She was.

And she'd blushed beautifully when she apologized for interrupting him, which was probably how she'd made it past Noreen, his queen-of-intimidation secretary.

Hollis had completely forgotten about the stacks of reports demanding attention on his desk, the sandwich he'd already had delivered for his lunch and the urge to upbraid Noreen for not rescheduling their appointment as she'd been instructed. For some insane reason, he'd wanted to be outside with Paige on that spectacular Vancouver summer day, somewhere close to the water with the sun glinting off that fabulous hair. And if he had to submit to the interview she'd requested concerning the article she was working on about the string of kidnappings among Canada's richest corporate families, so be it.

Hell, the idea that he could possibly be abducted like those four other executives had seemed so foreign to him at the time. Hollis had never been afraid for his personal safety a day of his life. He wasn't the type people messed with. He'd have laughed at the suggestion that three men could overtake him in broad daylight when he was jogging on the Stanley Park Seawall. Yet here he was hog-tied and wondering whether or not his family had forked over the ransom money his kidnappers had demanded.

He'd be damned surprised if they did. And this little road trip suggested they hadn't. His Uncle Luther and his cousins would consider it a family member's duty to sacrifice his own neck to save any portion of the Hollis corporate gains from being handed over to thugs. And he didn't expect his Aunt Evelyn to show any mercy either, even though she and Hollis's mother were fraternal twins.

He was done for.

The car stopped. Doors opened. He heard footsteps on gravel approaching the trunk. Heard the key turn in the lock. Felt a wave of fresh air bathe over his huddled form. He sucked it greedily through the velvet of the hood into his lungs as if it were a precious last gift. Hands grabbed him and roughly hoisted him out of the car. His bare thighs scraped painfully against the edge of the trunk.

"Over there, beneath those trees," a thin male voice said.

Hollis's heart pounded with fear of what was to come. He was helpless to change what would happen in the next few seconds or minutes, but he was determined to die with dignity and at peace with himself.

He closed his eyes and focused every ounce of his mental capacity on creating an image of Paige in his bed, her hair a resplendent halo capping her head. He imagined the vegetation brushing against him as he was carried toward the trees were Paige's light caresses. The swish of fabric rubbing against the thighs of the three men strong-arming him imitated the soft sounds she'd made as he'd plunged into her honeyed warmth, seeking acceptance and understanding and something more pure and powerful than the pursuit of greed. His chest swelled with gratitude that he'd met her, that she'd given him back some hope that the relationship between a man and a woman could be so soul-shattering, both physically and emotionally.

He was dropped unceremoniously on the ground. The dampness of the earth seeped through his T-shirt and running shorts.

This was it.

"I love you, Paige," he mouthed under his breath.

A boot slammed into his stomach like a pick. Then another.

Hollis tenaciously clung to his image of Paige and blanked out the pain.

"You're lucky, asshole," a gravely voice said. "We're lettin' you go. There's a knife within reachin' of your fingers. Whether you survive or not depends on you. Hell, we don't want a murder on our hands." His chortled laughter split the air.

Then a foot connected with Hollis's head, splintering his thoughts in a shower of stars.

Hollis didn't know how much time had passed before he came to. Minutes, maybe hours. He listened for sounds of voices, of danger, but all he could hear was the coarse caw of a raven and the sighing of branches in the wind.

He was alone. And alive.

For now.

His arms and legs were numb. Needles of pain streaked up his forearms as he flexed his fingers. But the hope of seeing Paige again, of having a future with her, gave him all the willpower he needed to keep himself from becoming coyote kibble.

He shifted his body and pawed the ground with his

head, finally succeeding in dragging off the black hood which had covered his head since his abduction. Blinking in the dappled sunlight, he rolled onto his stomach and lifted his head to scan the ground.

Relief flowed through him when he saw the hunting knife, the blade gleaming with the hope of salvation.

He rocked onto his side and blindly groped the ground for the knife, grunting when his fingers made contact with the handle.

Sweat beaded and dripped down his face as he rubbed the blade against the ropes binding his hands. It was a hell of a lot harder to do in real life than it looked in the movies, but Hollis would be damned if a dull blade would prevent him from being reunited with Paige.

He promised himself it would be a reunion both of them would never forget.

Chapter One

She was falling.

Paige Roberts awoke with a start, her heart pounding, her head throbbing, and the designer burgundy sheets twisted around her body. The queer sensation she was being hurtled through space toward a painful impact hovered on the edge of her consciousness and made a ridge of moisture bead along her spine.

Her fingers squeezed her pillow, seeking reassurance from its downy softness. She was safe. Stupid thing to dream about when she wasn't even going to be flying on her trip today. What time was it?

She propped open an eye and lifted her head to peer at the digital alarm clock on her bedside table, the small movement causing her brain to slam against the inside of her skull. The rods of light curling around the edges of the forest green mini blinds in her bedroom told her it had to be morning. 12:47? That couldn't be. She hadn't slept past noon since she'd been in university.

She gently let her head ease back into the indentation on her pillow, trying to remember what time she'd gone to bed last night. But her befuddled mind refused to dredge up an answer. Her throat felt raw and sore as if she'd spent the night before in the park cheering on her niece's soccer team, but she'd been too busy the last few days lining up some additional freelance assignments she could incorporate into this trip to indulge in the pleasure of encouraging a bunch of six-year-olds.

Paige closed her eyes and mentally counted to three before pushing herself out of the bed. Her arms ached, the muscles revolting against the movement. A wave of nausea leapt to her throat as she got to her feet. She braced her hands on the wall and hobbled toward the bathroom, veering around the suitcases heaped on the floor in front of her closet.

She never got sick. Somehow she must have picked up a nasty bug before a much anticipated five-week research trip across Canada. Maybe she should wait until tomorrow morning to take off, rather than leave today as she'd planned. She would still be able to make the scheduled interview in Ottawa for tomorrow afternoon.

The bathroom mirror bluntly informed her that she looked as awful as she felt and an extra day's rest would be well advised. The dark circles under her eyes resembled bruises.

She poked through her toiletries which were jumbled together in a floral travel bag plopped on the rim of the pedestal sink, ready to be thrown into her suitcase this morning, hoping to find a travel-size bottle of aspirin. No such luck. The medicine cabinet wasn't much help either; since she rarely got colds or headaches, it only contained extra soap and toothpaste.

She'd have to walk to the corner drugstore and pick something up. She splashed cold water on her face, pausing when she noticed a nasty scrape on the underside of her arm—just below her elbow—in her reflection in the mirror. Paige pushed back the sleeve of her Expos T-shirt and examined the scrape. Now how had that got there?

Had she scraped it piling her luggage and not noticed it? No, the scab didn't look that fresh. She reached for the towel and dried her hands, wincing as she realized the flu invading her body had the audacity to make her fingertips sore, too.

She could forget about the aspirin. What she needed was orange juice. Lots of it. And rest.

But her refrigerator and its tiny freezer compartment were bare. She'd done a good job of emptying both in preparation for her trip. Returning to her bedroom, she pulled a pair of black nylon jogging shorts out of her drawer, the very effort of putting them on exhausting her. Even her abdominal area was sore as if she'd forgotten to stretch out after a work-out. Bending over to tie laces required too much exertion, so she jammed her feet into an old pair of sandals. The pharmacy was across the street from the dépanneur, the corner market where she usually bought groceries. She didn't need to make a fashion statement. She ran her fingers through her fine blond hair, fluffing the easy-care layered cut, and grabbed her purse from its perch on top of her pile of luggage. She made a mental note that her laptop computer still needed to be added to the heap.

The humidity of a Montreal summer day sapped the strength from her bones as she carefully descended the steps of the oxblood brick semidetached house she rented in Outremont, near the University of Montreal. The shade of the trees lining the street granted some respite from the bright sunshine, but her head pulsed with a life of its own as though responding to the heat rising from the asphalt street.

The change in temperature as she entered the pharmacy made her dizzy, the icy blast of the conditioned air peppering her fair skin with goose bumps. Shivering, she hastily picked out aspirin and paid for her purchase. Her goose bumps stayed with her as she ventured out into the humidity again to cross the street to the dépanneur. A bell rang as she pushed open the door. The store was dark and close. Her stomach lurched at the smells of meat and cheeses at the deli counter. She filled a small wire basket with bottles of orange juice and apple juice, a fresh baked baguette and a cluster of bananas.

"Is that all?" the propriétaire inquired in French, punching numbers into the register.

Out of habit, Paige reached for a copy of *The Montreal Gazette* and added it to her purchases, answering automatically in French, "And this."

She glanced at the headline, her eyes narrowing on the date in disbelief. "What's the date today?" she demanded, wondering if her headache was affecting her vision.

"The fifteenth of July."

July fifteenth? Paige shook her head. No, it couldn't be. It was the fifth of June. She was leaving on her trip today.

"You okay, madame? You don't look so good."

Panic jangled through her bloodstream as she checked the front pages of the French dailies *La Presse* and *Le Devoir* just to be sure. Their mastheads insisted the date was July fifteenth.

"I'm fine. How much do I owe you?" she murmured weakly, opening her wallet. The compartment she reserved for keeping business receipts was jammed with folded slips of paper. She examined one as the owner hit the total button. It was a gas receipt for Sudbury, Ontario, dated July fourteenth.

How on earth could she have bought gas in Sudbury, Ontario at 6:47 p.m.? It was hundreds of kilometers away. She would have to have driven half the night to get from there to Montreal.

Her knees dipped. This couldn't be happening. What was going on?

Somehow, she found a twenty and thrust it at the owner, who looked at her as if she were sprouting two heads as he counted out change and loaded her purchases into white plastic bags.

Paige hurried out onto the sidewalk, the grocery bags jostling against her bare thighs. The heels of her sandals slapping sharply on the concrete. The quiet street seemed surreal, devoid of people and traffic. The sensation that invisible eyes were watching her from the black wrought iron balconies on the apartment buildings she passed made the hair rise on the back of her neck. She told herself she was being ridiculous. The street was quiet because people were at work or spending the week at their chalets in the Laurentians. The sound of a horn blaring on Avenue du Parc, two blocks down, made her jump.

Her next-door neighbor, sixty-two-year-old Audrey Lefebvre, was watering the vibrant purple and pink blooms of fuschia and impatiens brightening a turquoise planter suspended beneath her front window.

Paige didn't own plants, houseplants or otherwise. She had enough respect for all living things not to take on anything that couldn't survive a little neglect

when her mind was preoccupied with an article, and
that included pets, plants and boyfriends. Her contribution to keeping the small yard she shared with Audrey looking nice in the summertime was to push the
electric lawnmower around every week or so.

"Welcome home," Audrey exclaimed, setting her
old-fashioned tin watering can on the front stoop.
Tears blinked in Paige's eyes at the sight of Audrey's
familiar lined face, hunched shoulders and the sun-
flower print cotton apron she wore to keep her clothes
clean when she was tending her garden. "I was expecting you back days ago. How was your trip?"

"Exhausting," Paige said, blurting out the first
thing that came to mind. "I don't even know what
day it is."

Audrey chuckled and deadheaded a withering orange impatiens blossom. "Happens to me all the time
when I'm on vacation. It's July the fifteenth. The
Expos lost last night to the Blue Jays. And I piled up
the mail on your desk, just as you asked." Her blue
eyes twinkled behind narrow gold-rimmed bifocals.
"There were no big manila envelopes for you to
mope over either."

Great, Paige thought, she couldn't remember the
last five and a half weeks of her life, but at least she
was secure in the knowledge none of her articles had
been gathering rejection slips from editors across
North America.

"Thanks, Audrey. I owe you big time. I'd love to
stay and tell you about my trip, but I'm coming down
with some kind of bug and I need to lie down and
rest."

"Of course, dear. We'll talk when you're feeling
better. You do sound hoarse."

Paige let herself into her home and went straight down the hall to the kitchen, trying to absorb the fact that she, who'd always cast a skeptical eye on reports of alien abductions, was seriously considering it as a plausible explanation. Either that, or she'd fallen out of bed in the night and bumped her head.

She poured herself a big glass of orange juice and took a refreshing sip, then broke open the box containing the aspirin and attacked the safety seal around the neck of the bottle. The clear seal finally tore away and she opened the cupboard under the sink to toss it in the garbage. But the garbage can was already full of silvery blue silk.

Paige froze when she recognized the fabric of her favorite summer dress. What was it doing in the garbage? She couldn't remember throwing it away.

Frowning, she retrieved the dress, her eyes widening when she saw the rents in the fragile fabric and the dark stains. How on earth…? She held the fabric up to the strong afternoon sun streaming in the kitchen window to examine the stains on the skirt. Those stains looked like soil and…blood?

An almost unbearable slash of pain arced through her brain like lightning. Clammy perspiration beaded on her face as Paige felt her knees give out. In desperation, she grasped the edge of the ceramic counter to prevent herself from sinking to the floor. The dress landed on the counter's white tiles with a rattle.

A rattle?

Paige panted for breath and stared at the dress. The rattling sound it had emitted seemed as incongruous as the fact that her dress was ruined and she couldn't remember why. She poked the dress. Something rattled again.

She patted the silvery fabric and felt a small cylindrical shape concealed in a pocket. Her stomach churned with uneasiness as she extracted an unfamiliar bottle of prescription pills from the pocket. Her name was neatly typed on the label along with the date, July tenth. The pharmacy which had dispensed the drug had a Vancouver address. The doctor who'd issued the prescription was S. T. Locke.

Paige pressed her hand to her forehead as though trying to force herself to remember why a doctor, whose name didn't sound remotely familiar, would be giving her a prescription for painkillers with codeine. There was only one way to find out.

She reached for the phone and punched in the area code for Vancouver, then the pharmacy's number.

"Hi," she began unsteadily. "This is Paige Roberts, I had a prescription filled on July tenth."

She waited while the pharmacist pulled her file up on screen. "I have your file, ma'am, how can I help you?"

"I'm experiencing some unusual side effects to the medication that I would like to discuss with the doctor. I'm traveling and I realized his number was on the prescription form I gave you." She laughed with self-deprecation. "I don't seem to be thinking clearly these last few days. Would you mind giving me the number?"

"Of course, ma'am. Have you stopped taking the medication?"

"Yes."

"Good. Don't resume taking it until you've discussed the problem with your doctor. You can reach Dr. Locke at Vancouver General. Here's the number…"

Paige grabbed a pencil from an intricately carved wooden holder on the end of her kitchen counter and wrote the number on a notepad. Her fingers shook.

She thanked the pharmacist and hung up. Then summoned her courage and dialed the hospital. She endured ten anxious minutes on hold while Dr. Locke was paged. His voice had a mature brisk tone. She wished she could put a face to it.

Paige tried to keep a firm hold on her composure. "Dr. Locke, my name is Paige Roberts. I was recently a patient of yours and you gave me a prescription for painkillers on July tenth."

"Yes, I recognize your voice, Ms. Roberts."

"I'm glad to hear that. I know this will sound odd, doctor, but I don't remember you at all. I woke up this morning and I found this bottle of pills with your name on it." Her chin quivered. "C-could you tell me how I came to be under your care?"

"You were admitted to hospital with a head injury after you were injured in an explosion. You were here a couple of days under observation."

Relief that she wasn't crazy and that there was a logical explanation for her symptoms took the edge off her anxiety. "What type of explosion?"

"A car blew up." She sensed the doctor was choosing his words carefully. "You were in the wrong place at the wrong time. You were lucky you got off with a postconcussion headache and retrograde amnesia. When you came to, you didn't remember anything about the accident or how you came to be in B.C. But it sounds as if you're experiencing some anterograde memory loss, as well."

"What does that mean?"

"Loss of memory *after* the accident. And it should

certainly be looked into immediately. Are you experiencing any other symptoms?''

She described her headache and the nausea.

"Have you taken any of the pills?''

She opened the bottle and counted out the tablets. There were fifteen of them as indicated on the label.

"No, apparently not.''

"Where are you now, Ms. Roberts?''

"I'm at home in Montreal.''

"Do you know how you got home?''

Paige thought about the gas receipt from Sudbury. "I think I drove.''

Dr. Locke made a disapproving throat-clearing sound.

"I advised you not to drive home alone. But since you're home safely, we won't worry about that. I sent a note to your doctor to ensure you received some follow-up care. When you get off the phone, call your doctor and request an immediate appointment today. I'll be calling her to make sure she's heard from you. She'll probably want to run some tests. And *please,* don't drive. Get a family member or a friend to take you.''

Paige hung up the phone feeling even more scared.

In the end, she called a taxi and went to Dr. Garneau's office alone because she didn't want her sister or her parents to see the confused state she was in.

After examining her, her doctor sent her over to the hospital for a CAT scan.

"Well, good news,'' Dr. Garneau announced as she entered Paige's cubicle in the emergency room, her white coat flapping around her slender legs. A smile flickered on her lips. Paige didn't know how her doctor managed to care for her patients and mother the four kids whose grinning faces beamed at Paige from buttons pinned to Dr. Garneau's lapel.

Her fingers were warm and compassionate as she squeezed Paige's hand. "With your headache and the nausea, I was concerned there might be some bleeding into the brain, but there's no indication of that in the CAT scan. I think the combination of the accident and driving across Canada in five days has fatigued you and you really need to rest. I want to keep you here overnight for observation. I'll be in to check on you in the morning. If I think you're up to it, I'll send you home."

Paige let out the breath and the fears she'd been holding. "What about my memory? Will I get it back?"

"You should eventually. With posttraumatic amnesia, recovery of all memory in time is the rule, though, of course, there are always exceptions to any rule. With rest, the headaches and the nausea should go away and your memory will return. Just give it time."

Paige lifted her head off the pillow. "How much time?"

Dr. Garneau shrugged. "Who can say? Days maybe. Weeks. Months. What's important is that you're okay and there isn't a more serious injury going on."

Months!

Paige nodded and squelched a cry of protest as Dr. Garneau disappeared behind the pasty yellow curtain, leaving her alone. Unfamiliar noises and footsteps echoed around her. Paige nestled her head into the pillow and closed her eyes, comforting herself with the thought that she'd be home safe tomorrow.

"PAIGE, THANK HEAVENS you're back. I've been so worried. Why didn't you call me?"

Paige felt a rush of guilt at the concern and disappointment in Brenda Thompson's voice. She and Brenda had attended the same private school and grown up four mansions apart in Westmount. The exclusive mountainside city with British charm was perched on Mount Royal, whose treed slopes resembled the form of a slumbering giant in the center of Montreal's thriving metropolis.

Paige had been a witness at Brenda's wedding to Claude Belanger. She was the godmother of their son Alexandre, and she had comforted Brenda when Claude was kidnapped and murdered thirteen months ago. There had been three more kidnappings since Claude's, though Claude had been the only victim who'd been murdered. During her trip, Paige had planned to interview the surviving victims as well as executives of family-owned companies in hopes of discovering some common denominators that would help identify the kidnappers or suggest how they selected their victims.

"Sorry, Bren," Paige said. "You know what it's like when you come back after being away for so long. I'm swamped with mail and new assignments. And I've come down with a bug I can't shake, so I'm drinking orange juice and chicken soup and spending a lot of time in bed," she hedged, not wanting to divulge the real reason she hadn't returned Brenda's phone messages or the dozens of other messages left by her writing buddies and mother and sister on her answering machine. Everyone wanted to know about her trip and she didn't have a clue what to tell them. Paige had been sending them brief e-mail messages that she was swamped with deadlines and would call when she had time.

She'd been home just over two and a half weeks and her memory was as enlightening as a blank chalkboard.

Thanks to the Internet, she'd researched the different types of amnesia and felt reassured that since the CAT scan had shown no signs of permanent brain damage from a stroke or a bleed to the brain, her memory should eventually return—just as Dr. Garneau had said.

"I'm sorry to hear you're under the weather," Brenda murmured sympathetically. "I hope you'll be feeling up to speed soon. How was your trip? Did you manage to get all those articles done?"

"Yes, I got the assignments done," she said truthfully. Despite the fact that she had no idea what had happened to her laptop computer or her briefcase, which had contained all her interview notes and tapes, and her day planner, she'd been able to verify that she'd completed and e-mailed the work she'd been assigned to the respective editors. And they'd been able to provide her with backup copies.

Which was a relief, except that her research notes on the executive kidnappings had been in a file in her briefcase and she had little hope of retrieving them. Her best guess was that her laptop and her briefcase had been stolen from her car while she was in the hospital or at the scene of the accident.

The police officer she'd telephoned in Vancouver about the accident had been less than helpful with her inquiries. He'd been skeptical about her amnesia and she'd stopped phoning him out of sheer frustration. *How did she know she had her laptop with her or that it had been stolen from her car if she didn't remember? Maybe she'd left it elsewhere.*

The same officer expected her to call him immediately if she did regain her memory so he could take her eyewitness account of the accident.

Paige heard clanging in the background of the phone. Alexandre, Brenda and Claude's eighteen-month-old son, was obviously exploring the pots and pans cupboard again. Brenda raised her voice to be heard over her son's impromptu concert. "I just wanted to touch base with you about the other kidnapping. I wasn't sure if you'd heard about it while you were away," Brenda said, raising her voice.

Paige's heartbeat quickened. Another kidnapping?

"The victim's family contacted the police like I did when Claude was kidnapped," Brenda went on. "Apparently, the kidnappers released him unharmed, but they somehow learned the police were involved and they blew the victim up in a parking lot outside his office building when he returned to work after the incident."

Paige blanched, thinking of the victim's family. Of the grief Brenda was experiencing and would shoulder for the rest of her life. "Oh, my God. I had no idea, Brenda. But the families did the right thing to contact the police. It's the only way these people will ever be caught. You can't blame yourself for Claude's death. Even if you hadn't contacted the police, they might still have killed him just to show the rest of corporate Canada they mean business. So don't punish yourself."

"It's very hard not to." Pain and regret quavered in her friend's every word and brought hot, angry tears to Paige's eyes.

Paige gripped the phone tightly. "I understand. But Claude wouldn't want you to punish yourself. He'd want you to give all your emotional energy to taking care of Alexandre." She yanked a legal pad out of the third drawer of her desk to take notes, relieved she hadn't told Brenda of the underlying purpose for her research trip. "When did this happen?"

"A few weeks ago. He was abducted Canada Day weekend. Snatched when he was out jogging one morning. They held him for a couple of days, just like Claude. And he was left in an isolated wooded area after the ransom was paid." Brenda's voice cracked. "But instead of shooting him, they left him a knife to cut himself free. The poor guy managed to walk several kilometers and flagged down a car."

"Where was this? And what was the victim's name?"

"Vancouver. The victim was Hollis Fenton. The newspaper articles I have say he was the president of a shipping company. But his family owns a conglomerate with half a dozen operating companies in British Columbia, so he fits the profile. Wealthy enough to afford the ransom, but not so rich they'd hire body guards. Apparently he was a widower so he didn't have a wife and children."

Like Claude, Paige filled in silently. She stared at the notes she'd made. The name Hollis Fenton meant nothing to her. She couldn't recall whether or not it may have been on the handwritten list of names she'd drafted as possible interview subjects to contact when she was in Vancouver. Names she'd culled from profiles she'd clipped out of various business magazines and newspapers or from a handful of articles she'd found via the Internet. She had a backup file on the hard drive of her personal computer in her home office of information and theories relating to the four previous kidnappings and a proposal of how she'd like to present the information in an article. But she didn't have a backup of the articles themselves. Most of her information had been handwritten notes and clippings tossed into the file. She wished now she'd bothered to photocopy the contents of the file before she'd left.

The doorbell rang. "Can you fax the articles to me, Bren?" Paige said, walking into the hallway to answer the door. "I'd like to see them."

"Sure. Now, tell me about your trip. Did you meet any sexy males?"

"None worth remembering," she quipped with a wry smile. The doorbell gave a second insistent ring. Paige seized the excuse gratefully. "Listen, someone's at the door. I think it's a courier. I'll get back to you once I've read the articles, I promise."

She set her portable phone down on the narrow hall table and jerked the door open. The man occupying her front step was definitely memorable and sexy. But judging from the black T-shirt and black dress slacks that hung loosely on his athletic build, he was not a courier.

Whoever he was, he looked downright dangerous.

Chapter Two

Paige stared up into a no-nonsense face with a square-cut chin, a blunt nose and eyes as clear blue as a Laurentian lake. Closely shorn, sandy hair and a thin, two-inch scar slanting across his right temple, just above his eyebrow, gave his features a threatening cast.

Paige instinctively took a step backward.

"Paige?" he asked. The way he said her name gave her the oddest sensation she should know why he was standing on her doorstep. Should she?

Confusion paralyzed her tongue and she clung to the door in uncertainty as she felt his eyes rake over her white sleeveless top, khaki shorts and bare feet in a quick judgmental survey.

"Yes, I'm Paige Roberts," she managed to acknowledge.

After a moment's hesitation, he held out his hand. "I'm Matt Darby. I think you were expecting me? I came by to pick up the keys to Audrey's place."

Paige felt relief tumble through her and escape from her lungs with a short laugh as she accepted his proffered hand. "Of course. Sorry, I was in the middle of a call when you rang—you caught me with my mind elsewhere. You must be the nephew of Audrey's friend. Audrey talks about your aunt all the time, though I don't think she's mentioned you.''

''I'm one of a horde of nieces and nephews. We can't keep ourselves straight, much less expect anyone else to.''

The warmth and strength of his grip reached out to her, steadying her somehow. Making her feel stronger and more vibrant than she'd been in days. She loosened her hand from his reluctantly.

''Come in out of the heat. The keys are around here somewhere,'' she stammered, gesturing him to follow her into the hallway. ''Audrey was thrilled to have someone to pay the rent while she's off taking care of her sister in England.''

''Actually, she's doing me a favor, though I'm sorry her sister had to break her hip.''

She glanced back over her shoulder in time to see Matt grin. The crease deepening his cheek and the brilliant flash of white teeth completely transformed his expression. Made him seem more likeable, less dangerous. Paige tried to still the delicate flutters revolving in her stomach.

''Audrey didn't tell me much about you, except that you were coming to Montreal on business. What do you do?''

''I'm a headhunter,'' he said. His blue eyes settled lazily over her pale bare legs in a way that made the skin tingle on the back of her knees.

''I find qualified, experienced execs for corporations and businesses that are willing to pay top salaries for people who know their stuff.''

Which explained the way he'd sized her up immediately.

"How intriguing," she responded with a stern frown, briskly opening the beveled glass door to the small room she used as her office. Fortunately she was only his neighbor and not a job prospect so she didn't have to make a favorable impression beyond producing Audrey's keys. Now where had she put those keys? Aware that the backs of her knees were still tingling, Paige sifted through the piles of mail, magazines and files piled on her teak desk. Were Audrey's keys here on her desk? Or had she moved them to the kitchen?

She could sense Matt hovering in the doorway, watching her. "You don't sound intrigued," he said wryly.

Paige chuckled and glanced up from the desk, her eyes locking with his. For a second, the charisma of his personality pulled at her from across the room, as tangible as a faint tug on her arm. She had the feeling Matt Darby was very good at luring employees away from one company to work at another. Not to mention luring women out of their clothes. She shook her head as if resisting the pull and the dangerous bad-boy allure of that black T-shirt skimming well-developed pects and abs. "I'm willing to listen to anything while I hunt down these keys. I can't remember where I put them."

The fax machine on her credenza suddenly hummed to life, spitting the articles from Brenda into the tray. Paige moved aside a pile of papers mushrooming across her desktop, but Audrey's keys didn't magically appear. As she relocated a stack of research about amnesia, several pages escaped and drifted onto the floor.

Embarrassment seared through her as Matt bent down to help her collect them.

"It's okay, I've got it," she said, waving him away. "I've got a system and you'll mess it up."

A sandy brow jerked upward, doubting her. "Sure you do," he muttered skeptically, but he took the hint and backed off.

Color seeping into her cheeks, Paige scooped up the pages and laid them face down on top of the amnesia research. Her desk *did* have a system, but it seemed silly to debate the point with a stranger. The keys obviously weren't on the desk. Turning, she squinted at the wall of shelves loaded with books, periodicals and souvenirs from her travels. She dipped her fingers inside a Kundik clay mug she'd bought in Alaska and was rewarded with a thick layer of dust. Perplexed, she bit her lower lip and faced Matt.

"Maybe I put them in the kitchen. I'm sure it had to be somewhere I considered safe." Her cheeks grew even warmer as she met the unwavering intensity of his clear blue gaze. "Sorry, I get a little distracted sometimes when I'm working and I forget things."

His gaze drifted to the clutter heaped around the computer on her desk as if he knew she hadn't done anything that could be described as real work for the last two and a half weeks, but he gave her a polite smile.

"So, how do you earn an honest buck?" he asked as she slipped past him into the hallway.

"I'm a freelance journalist." Her eyes swept the antique pine sideboard centered in front of her living room window and the leather-topped stack of books that was her coffee table for the glimmer of brass keys as they passed.

Matt, she noticed, seemed to be studying the eclectic mix of watercolors and oils dotting the hunter green walls of her living room.

Paige headed down the hallway to the kitchen. In exchange for some advertorials and press releases, a decorative artist had glazed the walls and the ceiling with a warm mustard color to create an old-world "Italian villa" feel to match the outdated cupboards and appliances.

The keys were nowhere in sight.

Paige opened a glass-fronted upper cabinet where she kept a few pieces of china and crystal and sighed as she lifted down a gold-rimmed teacup. The diamond earrings her grandmother gave her when she graduated from journalism school were nestled inside, wrapped in tissue, but no keys.

"Can I offer you a drink?" she asked Matt, straight-faced. "We could be here a while. There's juice, lemonade, soda, beer?"

"A beer sounds good. It's hot out and I've been in traffic most of the day. I drove up from Ottawa."

She opened the refrigerator, standing on tiptoe to see if she'd left the keys on top of it, then passed him a bottle of beer. "Is that where you're from, Ottawa?'

He shrugged, his mouth drawing into a tight line. "Most recently. I've lived in so many places I don't consider myself from anywhere anymore." He took a long swallow of beer.

Paige found her gaze lingering on the masculine bobbing of his throat muscles.

Get a grip! She told herself firmly, thinking her

amnesia was seriously affecting her brain cells. She tugged open the drawer nearest the back door. She'd been in the kitchen when Audrey had dropped by and told her she had to leave suddenly because her sister in England had fallen and injured herself. She'd given Paige the keys and a box of plant fertilizer...and a list of plants to water.

"What about your family?" she asked Matt. "Where are they?"

"Out west mostly. We're not that close."

He put his hand on the face of the drawer she was rummaging through and abruptly changed the subject. Paige noticed his lean fingers had small pink scars on them.

"Maybe if you told me what the keys looked like I could help you look," he offered.

"They're two ordinary brass house keys on a silver ring. Try under the sink. There's a plastic holder for grocery bags. Audrey gave me a bag containing soluble plant fertilizer for her window box. Maybe the keys were in the bag and I didn't notice."

"I'll check the bags in the holder."

"Thank you. I'll check the bathroom. Audrey gave me a watering can, too. Since I don't see it here in the kitchen, I might have put the fertilizer and the watering can in the linen closet in the bathroom."

Her hunch was correct. What's more, she found the keys inside the watering can. Thank heavens! She was growing worried she'd have to offer to put Matt up on her couch until she'd found them.

"Voilà," she announced, practically waltzing into the kitchen. He didn't seem to notice her until she tapped him on the shoulder, wiggling the keys under his nose as he turned to look at her.

"Don't ask me where I found them. I'm embarrassed enough already."

Matt's fingers closed around the keys and her fingers. His blue eyes were clouded with concern and perhaps something else she didn't want to acknowledge. "Are you okay?" he asked.

Had he been close enough to read the articles in her office? Close enough to put two and two together?

Her legs trembled and the temptation to tell him—to tell someone other than her doctor—about her amnesia hovered on the tip of her tongue. But Matt would think she was a lunatic if she did. He probably already thought she was a lunatic.

She forced a false, bright smile. "Sure, I'm fine. Just forgetful. If you need anything let me know. I'll be happy to tell you where the stores are and where to catch the bus and the metro."

"Thanks. I'll take you up on that offer."

Which sounded like a promise. For a second he stared down at her, his expression fiercely intense and Paige had the distinct feeling he might actually be thinking about kissing her, which seemed ridiculous considering they'd met fifteen minutes ago. But her fingers curled into her damp palms at the alarming possibility and her heart thudded unsteadily against her sternum.

Then he blinked, shattering her impression as his expression shifted into neutral. He retreated toward the back kitchen door, leaving her feeling unsettled and oddly disappointed. "I'll let myself out here if you don't mind. My car's parked in the rear by the garage anyway."

"Sure." Paige locked the screen door behind him,

watching for a minute as he strolled confidently over to Audrey's back stoop and tried the keys in the door. It would be nice to hear the sounds of another person inhabiting the other half of the semidetached. She'd felt even more isolated since Audrey's abrupt departure. And maybe she could pick his brain about the kidnappings. A headhunter would probably have a lot of specialized information about corporations and know which ones were family owned.

Which reminded her that Brenda's fax awaited her in her office. Giving Matt's athletic build a last wishful and appreciative glance, she headed back to her office.

Brenda had sent a dozen articles from *The Globe and Mail, The Montreal Gazette,* and two British Columbia newspapers, *The Vancouver Sun* and *The Province.*

Gathering up the faxes, a pen and the legal pad she'd made notes on earlier, she settled into her favorite reading chair—a worn olive velvet wing chair that had been her grandmother's—and arranged the articles by date from Fenton's abduction, to his release, to the explosion which took his life. The first article was dated July seventh, but the kidnapping had taken place on July third. The family had obviously managed to keep it out of the paper until the victim had been released.

Shipping Exec Held Hostage, the headline blazed on the first article from *The Vancouver Sun.* She read the details of Hollis Fenton's early Saturday morning abduction by three armed men wearing dark ski masks and driving a gray sedan. He was held in what he thought was a house and released late Tuesday in Mount Seymour Park after the ransom was paid. Unlike the previous kidnappings, Fenton's precise release location was not revealed to the family and police began a wide-scale search of wooded areas in the Vancouver region. It was nearly ten o'clock before Fenton had freed himself from his bindings and descended the mountain road to reach help. Police were asking anyone who may have seen anything suspicious to contact them.

Two of the other articles listed the same details, but added information about the victim's family. Not surprisingly, since three of the other four victims were company presidents, Hollis Fenton was president of Pacific Gateway Shipping, one of several companies held by the Hollis Group, which was headed up by Luther Hollis, Hollis Fenton's uncle. There was speculation that Hollis Fenton, who was widowed two years ago after his wife's tragic suicide, was selected because his six cousins who operated various other Hollis-owned enterprises from insurance and financial services, to accounting firms and real estate management companies, were married and/or had children.

Paige ruminated about this for a while, then moved on to the other articles. Execs Under Seige contained security tips and estimates about the ransom amounts demanded by the kidnappers. Claude had been kidnapped on a Monday and one million dollars had been asked for. But the kidnappers hadn't collected it at the drop-off site.

She frowned and made a note about the day of the week the kidnapping occurred on her legal pad. Why a Saturday? She had no idea when the kidnappers alerted the family with the ransom demand, but why kidnap someone on a Saturday when most Canadian banks were open limited hours—usually from 10 a.m. to 2 p.m.? Brenda had told her it usually took two or three business days for a financial institution to fulfill a request for a large cash withdrawal. The cash had to be ordered and delivered by armored guard.

With the exception of Hollis Fenton, the other victims were abducted on a Monday or Tuesday. Why the change to Saturday when the family might be forced to wait until Monday morning to approach the bank? It seemed counterproductive to the kidnappers' objectives. Had the kidnappers deliberately anticipated that anxiety, the building frustration of being unable to act? She shuddered at the thought.

The next article and accompanying photo brought tears to her eyes when she read the headline, Released To Die: Cruel Bomb Takes Exec's Life. It was easy to imagine the victim's relief at being freed, the joy of returning to his life, only to have it cruelly blow up around him as he'd arrived to work his first morning back. A bomb planted in a stolen car in the parking lot had been ignited as he'd walked past. As the photo of Pacific Gateway Shipping's offices indicated, metal debris from the car had flown everywhere and windows had shattered in buildings within a block radius. Hollis Fenton had died at the hospital. The early hour of the explosion had prevented others from being killed, though several minor injuries were reported, and a young unidentified woman was taken to the same hospital unconscious.

Paige stiffened as a hunch stirred the fine hair on her neck. *A young, unidentified woman?* She checked the date Brenda had scrawled beside the headline. July eighth.

She'd been released from the hospital July tenth!

No wonder that damn police officer wanted her to call him when she regained her memory! She pulled her knees up to her chest, capturing the article against her heart as she rocked back and forth. She was a journalist. If she was in Vancouver when the kidnapping had occurred, there was a good chance she'd decided to lurk outside Fenton's office in hopes of getting an interview. Nausea rose sharply in her throat. Paige leapt from her chair, scattering papers everywhere, and ran to the bathroom to empty her stomach in the toilet.

Was it possible she'd witnessed Hollis Fenton's murder?

Chapter Three

With his good ear, Hollis listened to the toilet flush and the water running through the pipes next door and closed his eyes, leaning his forehead against the wall. Paige was there next door. She hadn't recognized him.

Which had been the point of the colored contact lenses and the drastic haircut that still made him grimace when he looked in the mirror. The barber's razor had removed the thick sun-streaked layer that had earned him the nickname "Golden Boy" from his cousins, leaving this duller nondescript base. A makeover artist had spent forty-five minutes reshaping his brows and plucking away any telltale lighter strands. Those changes combined with a broken nose and the twelve pounds he'd dropped while in the hospital recovering from a punctured lung, had altered his appearance to the point where he barely recognized his bony-faced reflection. All he needed was army fatigues to look like a battle-scarred army sergeant. Still, it was better than dead. Even if he'd be permanently deaf in his left ear.

But he'd hoped—no, he'd expected—Paige to recognize him. He'd expected to see that same wide, joyous smile that had sent him sprinting toward her the instant he'd spotted her across the street. With every fiber in his being, Hollis wanted to believe that smile had saved his life—despite what the police were speculating.

Every beat of his heart rejected the idea that the woman he'd yearned to hold in his arms this afternoon had betrayed him in thought, word and deed. Contriving the interview…sleeping with him… learning the details of his schedule to set up his abduction, then conveniently coming down with amnesia.

But doubts racked Hollis's mind. How else could the kidnappers have known his family had contacted the police? Only his family and Noreen had known the police were involved. But Paige had pried the information out of Noreen. Noreen's word—*pried.*

Then there was the unsettling fact that Paige hadn't wanted to come see him at his uncle's house after his release. Her soft, urgent insistence on a private meeting had warmed his blood, kindling his need to be with her. His family hadn't known about their relationship so he'd agreed and suggested they meet early in the lobby of his shipping office. He figured he'd check his desk, exert his presence and authority in case his Aunt Evelyn or his cousin Sandford had staged a coup in his absence, then play hooky with Paige for the rest of the day—preferably in his bed.

But why had she walked over from her hotel, rather than drive over? Had she known about the bomb planted in the trunk of the stolen car parked in his lot? Had she known not to come too close?

The file Noreen had found in Paige's briefcase when she'd retrieved her belongings at the hotel was the real kicker, though. Hollis felt physically ill just thinking about that file and the information it contained about the other kidnappings. Inside information that had never made it into the newspapers—including a cryptic list that matched the modus operandi of his abduction. Then there was the diskette containing all those interview notes with a criminologist and other executives like him. Maybe it was all legit and she was just one hell of an investigative journalist.

Maybe not.

He hadn't shared either with the police, yet. But he wouldn't hesitate to do so if he determined Paige's amnesia story was a ruse and she'd betrayed him. He'd told the police he'd stay out of sight until it was safe to reveal he was alive; he just hadn't told them he planned on hiring a private investigation firm to make Audrey Lefebvre an offer she couldn't refuse so he could move next door to Paige. If the Montreal police had her under surveillance, they'd never know who he was.

Hollis ran his fingers over the cabbage rose wallpaper as though feeling for a pulse of Paige's presence next door. The memory of his first marriage made his fingers tremble. He'd fallen for a woman's lies once. He'd thought he'd known Christine, known the kind of woman she was. But she'd fooled him. Badly.

Paige had seemed shaken this afternoon and downright secretive about those papers on her desk. He didn't know what to think about those damn keys. Had that been an act or the real thing? The woman he'd fallen in love with had been radiant, confident and organized, but the Paige he'd met today had been pale, uncertain and nervous.

Fear had tarnished her silver gaze, making him wonder just what the hell she was afraid of—not recovering her memory? Or being caught?

Hollis planned on becoming intimately involved in her life until he found out.

THE SIGHT OF PAIGE'S blond head peering through the front window halted Hollis in his tracks as he walked barefoot down Audrey's gleaming oak hallway, a mug of instant coffee in one hand, a map of Montreal in the other. What the hell was she doing? Spying on him?

He'd thought to sit out on the front steps to acquaint himself with his new surroundings and plot a few coincidental meet-Paige encounters. But if she was going to make it easy for him by spying through his windows, he'd take her up on it.

He quietly released the dead bolt and slipped outside onto the front steps, the cement cool on the soles of his bare feet. Paige's derriere, in crisp navy shorts, presented an attractive view as she leaned over the window box. Her hair was loosely clipped up off her neck, wayward strands of sunshine tumbling over a silver barrette.

She was definitely a Peeping Tom.

"Morning, neighbor," he said briskly, enjoying her guilty start of surprise.

As she whirled around, an arc of water splashed from the spout of the tin watering can she held and landed on his toes. Color as vibrant pink as the flowers she'd obviously been watering suffused her cheeks. "Oh, good morning. You startled me." She pressed her free hand to her heart, leaving a smear of potting soil on the tempting full upper curve of her right breast.

Hollis eyes narrowed on the stain, his fingers curling tightly around the handle of the ceramic mug. While he couldn't see Paige's heart thundering beneath the clinging pale green knit top, he knew it was thundering because he could see the rapid rise and fall of her rib cage. Was she peering in his window because she was suspicious of him?

"We're even," he said mildly. "Audrey didn't tell me one of the perks of this location was that I'd have the flattering attention of an attractive neighbor."

She flushed even pinker, that same damn beautiful flush which had landed him hook, line and sinker the day she'd sauntered into his office. It still got to him. "I was just checking to see if you were up yet. I thought I'd invite you in for breakfast or a coffee if you didn't bring supplies with you." She gestured toward his English china mug emblazoned with a thatched Tudor pub. "But I see you found coffee."

"That's about all I found in the cupboards. Instant coffee, tea bags, oatmeal and mountains of sugar and ketchup packets from McDonalds."

Paige laughed, the tinkling sound filling the empty hollowness in his chest. "That sounds like Audrey. She eats out a lot with her friends and thriftily helps herself to freebies. But she rarely goes out for breakfast because she says she can't start her day without a bowl of porridge and a cup of tea. The instant coffee is for her friends who don't drink tea." She clutched the watering can to her chest and met his gaze with almost ingenuous trust. But the violet half moons under her eyes indicated something was

weighing heavily enough on her mind—or her conscience—to keep her up at night. "So what do you
say to toast or a fried egg to go with that coffee?"
she added.

Hollis sternly reminded himself that Christine had
concealed her bipolar illness behind a face that had
seemed to glow with her uncontainable enthusiasm
for life. The euphoria which accompanied her every
action, from lovemaking to traveling to shopping, had
been a symptom of her manic-depressive illness.
He'd learned after they were married just how dramatically her mood could alter. He'd often come
home to find her sitting in their darkened bedroom in
her pajamas, unable to move for days, sometimes
weeks at a time. Anger that she hadn't told him about
her illness before they were married warred con-
stantly with his grief over her suicide. Maybe if he'd
handled things differently when she'd abducted a
newborn infant from the hospital to prove to him she
was capable of raising a family, she'd still be alive.
She'd been arrested and admitted to a hospital for
psychiatric assessment. He'd been so afraid of what
might happen next that he'd threatened her with a
divorce if she didn't take her prescribed medication.

"I'm game for breakfast," he replied. "In fact,
your timing couldn't be better." He held up the map
of the city.

"My immediate order of business is to find a grocery store and a bank machine."

"Fortunately, I eat and I'm dependent on banks as
much as the next person, so I can help you with both
requests. Why don't you lock up and meet me at my
place in a few minutes? And bring the map with you.
I'll start some eggs."

''Thanks.'' How did she do that? Hollis wondered as he entered Audrey's half of the semidetached. In the blink of an eye, Paige had made him feel comfortable with her as if they'd spent years together. His jaw clenched as he stalked upstairs to Audrey's bedroom in search of his runners.

Twenty seconds later he was on her front steps. She'd left the door open for him. He rapped politely on it.

The smell of fresh-brewed coffee greeted him, along with the hospitable beckoning warmth of Paige's voice that seemed to chide him for ever believing she could be involved with kidnappers and murderers. ''I'm back in the kitchen.''

As he walked down the hall he noticed that the door to her office was closed, but the beveled panes of glass allowed him to note her desktop was noticeably cleaner this morning. The big stack of papers she hadn't wanted him to see yesterday was gone. So much for thinking up an excuse to sneak in there for a look.

Paige was frying eggs at the stove and humming along to the radio. She had already set the bistro-size ash and metal table for two and poured grapefruit juice into glasses. A couple of the flowers she'd been watering had been plopped into a crystal bud vase. The scene hit Hollis with the impact of a fist in the stomach. It was so painfully close to what he wanted from her and yet probably not real, all at the same time. His fingers slid, damp with perspiration, on the map he was holding.

She glanced over her shoulder at him with a smile. ''Make yourself at home. Two eggs fine for you?''

Hollis nodded, speechless, greedily soaking up the

brightness of her eyes and the generous curve of her mouth. His body went rigid with desire. Surreptitiously covering himself with the map, he sat down before he could embarrass himself further.

"You're treating me well for a stranger." He took a sip of the juice.

"You're not exactly a stranger…more like a friend of a friend, *n'est-ce pas?*" She slid the eggs onto his plate with a spatula. Hollis stilled as she hesitated, her light citrusy scent teasing his appetite, her pale silken legs within inches of his touch. "But you're right, I do have a hidden agenda."

"You do?" he croaked, nearly coughing up the grapefruit juice.

She nodded. "Actually, I have two of them, but I'll start with the easy one first."

He eyed her with deep-rooted suspicion as she deposited the frying pan in the sink and pulled four slices of whole wheat toast from her toaster oven. "Should I eat first or wait for the first revelation?"

She put two slices of toast on his plate. "Eat first. My sister tells me it's easier to get something out of someone if they're fed and satisfied."

Satisfied? After three weeks of missing her, wanting her so badly he couldn't sleep, Hollis was so strung out with tension that two eggs and toast couldn't begin to satisfy him. He jabbed his fork into an egg and took a bite to prevent himself from telling her just that.

Paige set a steaming cup of black coffee near his elbow, along with a sugar bowl and creamer, then sat down across from him to spread something that looked like chocolate on her toast.

"What is that?" he asked.

She flashed him a sunny grin. "A culinary idiosyncrasy of Quebec. Try some. It's a hazelnut spread with cocoa."

Dubious, Hollis dabbed a small amount on the corner of his toast and took a bite. It was a little sweet for this early in the morning, but good.

Even though he thought he knew the answer, he asked anyway, "Are you from here originally?"

"Born and raised. My mother's family came here in the 1840s fleeing the potato famine in Ireland. My dad's family is from the Ottawa Valley. He retired last year from men's retail clothing. My mom is a jewelry designer."

Hollis breathed a little easier. She hadn't added that her father had chosen retirement over bankruptcy and closed his custom men's clothing store. However, her story was consistent with what she'd told him in Vancouver—and she looked so damn honest when she spoke. But then, the presence of her knees lodged a hairbreadth from his under the small table was preventing him from thinking straight.

"Have you been to Montreal before?" she asked.

He nodded, soaking up the remaining yolk on his plate with a piece of his toast. "A few times, but I've flown in and relied on taxis to get around." Actually, he and Christine had spent a whirlwind few days soaking up the culture and the cuisine. A frown tugged at the corners of his mouth as he remembered the extravagant shopping spree that had sparked one of their first arguments. It seemed such a long time ago. He was older, now. Wiser. He wouldn't make the same mistake.

"Enough distracting small talk, Ms. Roberts," he

said gruffly. "Spit out the first item on your agenda. I'm all ears."

She blushed and brushed the crumbs from her fingers.

"Okay, here it is. Do you have a green thumb?"

"I beg your pardon?"

"A green thumb. Audrey's only been gone a week and her flowers are wilting under this heat wave. She's counting on me to look after her garden and I know I'm going to disappoint her. I'm a repeat offender when it comes to killing plants." Her eyes glowed with dry candor. "Any chance I can entice you to take over—or, at the very least, remind me to water?"

Hollis stroked his jaw, studying her. He hadn't shaved this morning and the stubble rasped against his palm. "Hmm...Now, that's an interesting proposal. Just what kind of enticing did you have in mind?"

She colored to the tips of her ears. "Neighborly favors of a platonic nature."

He raised his eyebrows. "Ah, hence the desire to give me directions to the grocery store."

"Precisely. I'm desperate."

"So there's room to negotiate?"

Her eyes narrowed and Hollis thought she should be able to see beneath the billiard-ball haircut, the misshapen nose and the scar. *See him.* His gut clenched. She was either a superb actress or genuinely had amnesia. He prayed for the latter.

"Are you trying to drive a hard bargain?" she asked.

"Sorry, it's second nature to me."

"I'm afraid to ask my other favor."

"Don't be."

"I am."

Their gazes locked for a moment and Hollis lost himself in the shadowed layers of reluctance and fear that lurked in the silvery depths. *Trust me,* he wanted to say.

Paige ducked her head and put her chocolate toast down as if she'd suddenly lost her appetite. "I think, I'll save it for a couple of days and try again."

"And keep me in suspense?"

"Yes." She rose and reached for his plate.

He gripped the edge of the trendy designer plate, stopping her. "Now who's driving a hard bargain?"

"You haven't seen the way I give directions yet."

He snorted and let go. He'd seen her day planner and had spent hours sightseeing with her. He knew she was a detail-oriented person. He rose and helped clear away the dirty glasses, setting them on the counter. "May I ask you something?"

"You can try."

Hollis felt a slow grin ease over his face. He'd been in her home twenty minutes and she was already completely under his skin, the sexual tension escalating between them as rapidly as the words they were exchanging. "Are you seeing someone right now?"

"Only the guy in my kitchen."

He gritted his teeth. "I meant, are you dating anyone at the moment?"

"No." She turned the tap on and squirted liquid dish detergent into the sink.

"Good."

She looked up at him, her expression guarded, uncertain. "Good?"

He let his gaze skim over the tiny golden freckles dusting her arms and the pert feminine thrust of her breasts before settling on her moist, slightly parted lips. *How could she not know him?* ''Yes, good. Because then you can meet me in Audrey's garden every evening and we'll look after it together.''

''Oh, good.'' She turned quickly back to the sink, a tide of pink appearing from beneath the collar of her top and spreading up her neck.

Hollis was tempted to trace the sensitive skin of her nape with his tongue. The last time he'd done that she'd reacted by wiggling her derriere into his hips and complained he was giving her goose bumps. His voice came out strained. ''Maybe I can convince you to ask your other favor.''

''All in good time, Matt. Get your map.''

Hearing his assumed name on her lips doused his ardor like salt water on a bonfire. He promised himself, that all in good time, she'd know exactly who he was.

If she didn't suspect already.

SIX DAYS LATER, Paige stared at a chart of the circulatory system posted on the wall in Dr. Garneau's examination room and wondered why her memory was taking so long to recover. It had been thirty-two days since the explosion and she wasn't sure she was making any progress. Maybe it was the worry that she may have met with Hollis Fenton and learned something important from him about his kidnapping, which caused the lingering fatigue and the nausea.

The headaches, as Dr. Garneau had suggested, had faded and were only resurrected when she tried to force herself to remember something about the miss-

ing weeks of her life. She'd even refrained from asking Matt for his input on the kidnappings for fear it
would cause another headache like the brain-splitter
she'd gotten when she'd returned Brenda's call about
the articles.

Instead, she'd concentrated on being a good patient. Going to bed early. Trying to eat well. Taking
it easy by working on general interest filler pieces for
magazines. And spending far too much time sassing
back and forth with Matt in Audrey's garden every
evening as they weeded, watered and deadheaded the
flowers in the perennial border.

Paige closed her eyes and imagined Matt's hard-
edged good looks. He'd been a much needed distraction the last week; she could relax around him because he had no idea of her memory loss. The fact
she found him attractive, stimulating and easy to talk
to, was an added bonus. It had been a long time since
she'd been interested in a man. But her constant fatigue and another bout of nausea had forced her to
turn down Matt's impromptu dinner invitation Saturday night.

At least he'd been gracious about her refusal. But
the desire to be well again and have the stamina to
show Matt all the hot Montreal nightspots—if he
asked her out again—sent her back to the doctor
when she woke up this morning with a queasy stomach.

Dr. Garneau gave her a complete physical exam,
asked her a barrage of personal questions including
whether or not she was involved with anyone, and
took blood and urine samples. Then she asked Paige
to get dressed and wait for a few minutes.

Paige fiddled with the top button of her lemon silk

dress. She started as a sharp rap sounded on the door
to the examining room and Dr. Garneau came in,
Paige's chart clasped in her hands. Something about
Dr. Garneau's subdued expression caused Paige's
stomach to knot in alarm.

"I have an explanation for your symptoms,
Paige," Dr. Garneau told her quietly, without pre-
amble. "You're pregnant."

Chapter Four

Paige gasped. *Pregnant!*

"Are you sure?" she stammered. "How could I be? I haven't, I mean...I haven't been with anyone since... I've been irregular before...." she said, hoping this was a big mistake.

"I'm positive. You gave me the date of your last cycle in May. You're probably five to seven weeks along."

Five to seven weeks?

Paige's body swayed.

Dr. Garneau moved quickly. "Easy. Lean forward and put your head between your knees. I know this is a shock."

A shock was an understatement. Paige put her hand on her belly and drew a deep breath in, then exhaled slowly. A baby, part her, part some stranger she couldn't even remember, was growing in her.

Who had fathered it?

Suddenly she remembered the torn dress she'd found in her kitchen garbage can and the soreness of her body the morning she'd awoken to having no memory. She'd felt bruised and battered. Yes, those injuries could have been a result of being caught in the explosion. But a horrible alternative congealed in her conscious mind. She looked up at Dr. Garneau with wide eyes and wished she hadn't thrown out the dress.

"Is it possible I was raped?"

"What makes you think that?" Dr. Garneau asked.

Paige told her about the dress. "Since I'd found the painkillers in the pocket of the dress, I just assumed I'd been wearing it when the explosion occurred, but what if I wasn't? What if I was wearing the dress on the drive back to Montreal and something horrible happened to me? Maybe the shock of what I'd been through made me vulnerable to someone and I've blocked it out along with the other details about my trip."

Paige tried to draw reassurance from the calming stroke of Dr. Garneau's hand on her shoulder and the soothing tones of her voice. "I understand your fears, Paige, but it's too soon to reach any conclusions. I gave you a complete physical when you came to my office that day and I didn't find any evidence to suggest you'd been sexually assaulted."

"Well, this baby wasn't immaculately conceived," Paige muttered biting down on her lip in dismay. A baby! Judging from her sister's discourses on the joys of motherhood and Brenda's experience trying to raise a baby on her own, Paige knew nurturing a child was in a league of its own—well above plant tending and pet caring. What would her parents say when she informed them she was going to be a single mother?

Paige hugged herself tightly. It didn't matter what anyone said. Regardless of the circumstances of its conception, this was her baby and she was prepared to love it and raise it to the best of her ability—even if the prospect of doing something wrong terrified her. But for her own peace of mind, she needed to put a name and a face to the man who had given her this keepsake.

One-night stands weren't in her nature, but maybe she'd met someone irresistible...and maybe she should try writing fiction instead of nonfiction, she scoffed, giving herself a mental shake. "What if I tried to retrace the steps of my trip?" she asked her doctor. "Do you think it might stimulate my memory?"

"I think it would be ill-advised for the time being—especially when you don't know what you could be walking into."

Fear nagged on the fringes of Paige's heart.

"I'm going to refer you to a psychiatrist who'll help you figure out what's going on. I'll pull a few strings and see if we can't get you an appointment ASAP."

Paige left the doctor's office feeling overwhelmed and alone. She was even more depressed when her doctor's office called later that afternoon to tell her they'd been lucky enough to book an appointment with the psychiatrist in two weeks.

Paige supposed she should feel grateful, but two weeks seemed like an interminable time to wait for answers.

"HEY, ANYONE HOME? You're not flaking out on me already are you, Paige?"

The sound of Matt's deep voice drifting through her home pierced the chaotic confusion of Paige's thoughts and brought her sharply back to earth.

"I'm here," she said, pushing herself out of her

grandmother's wing chair. She'd spent the last couple of hours, curled in that chair, her arms wrapped protectively around her midriff, trying to adjust to the fact that she was going to have a baby.

A glance in the hall mirror told her she looked a mess.

She tucked her hair behind her ears and hoped Matt wouldn't notice she'd been crying.

His tall, lean form filled the frame of the screen door, the inherent strength his broad shoulders offered compelling her to hurry.

"It's about time. I was worried I'd have to storm your kitchen and throw you over my shoulder to force you to hold up your end of the bargain."

Paige laughed, her fingers trembling as she unlocked the screen door. "I warned you it could come to that." She glanced up into his face and her breath caught in her throat. For some reason she felt grounded when her eyes met his steady blue gaze— and she felt something else: a spark of undeniable attraction that heated her skin and brought a flush to her cheeks.

Matt gave her a lazy grin. "I would hardly think a feminist like you would let a man sweep her off her feet."

"You're right. I wouldn't," Paige fired back. But she had to admit, the idea had a primitive appeal— particularly if Matt was doing the carrying. She had no idea how a man could look as if he belonged on the cover of a business magazine and wild at the same time. She recognized the labels on the navy shorts and the print golf shirt he wore. They were the best money could buy, but they hung loosely on his frame as if he didn't give a damn. And the way he'd been using the backyard for an office, reading the business sections of the financial newspapers and working on his laptop computer suggested he preferred the outdoors to a conventional office. Paige suspected he was a maverick through and through.

''Were you working?'' he asked as she stepped out onto the back stoop.

The humidity seemed to sap the strength from her bones. Or was it her proximity to Matt? ''Not really. Just brainstorming.''

''Have you eaten?''

Paige shook her head. ''It's too hot to cook. I'll eat something later.''

''Well, I haven't eaten yet either. Why don't I take you out to dinner when we're finished? One of my client's suggested a restaurant in Old Montreal that specializes in seafood and bluepoint oysters. I thought we could give it a try.''

He must mean Gibby's, her favorite restaurant, which was located in a two-hundred-year-old stable. Normally, she adored seafood, but her stomach lurched in rebellion at the prospect. Paige tried to hide her reaction and disengage herself from the blatant interest in Matt's eyes. Her sense of timing couldn't be worse. It had been a long time since she'd felt this kind of mercurial chemistry for anyone...but the baby made everything so complicated. She had too many problems to be sidetracked by Matt's flattering attention. She owed it to herself and to the baby to find her baby's father.

She stared at a navy button on his shirt—the only thing on his person that didn't radiate male sexuality. ''I'm not sure I'm up to a dinner out. I'm still feeling really tired.''

Hollis steeled himself against the annoyance caused by her rejection. What was the matter with her? She was positively pale. Was it possible part of her memory was returning and she'd remembered him? Was mourning his death? She jumped a few inches off the doormat when he touched her arm. "Maybe you should rest then," he offered. "I'll take care of the garden tonight."

"No, I'll help. A deal's a deal." She lifted her head, her hair shifting in golden strands around her thin face.

Hollis's heart twisted with agony when her eyes lingered on his mouth. He'd have handed over his retirement fund to know what she was thinking.

"Besides," she added, "it feels good to be outside."

"How about we compromise and I'll have something delivered? We can eat on Audrey's patio under the trees where it's cool."

"Deal. But only if you order Chinese. I'm in the mood for rice and stir-fried vegetables."

Hollis laughed. "Your wish is my command."

"Those are dangerous words, mister, and could get you in a lot of trouble. I have very expensive tastes."

Every ounce of testosterone in his body leapt to awareness at her challenge. Hollis wet his lips and planted his arms on the black wrought iron porch rail behind her, effectively trapping her. Her expressive silver eyes widened as he lowered his head until they were nearly nose to nose. Her sweet breath fanned his mouth and tickled his cheek. Heat and need combusted into flames in Hollis's body. "I recognized you for trouble the minute you plied me with breakfast and offered me a position as chief gardener," he rasped, nearly drunk on the overwhelming rush of being this close to kissing her. "Which reminds me, I'm still waiting to hear what that second favor is. Care to share?"

"N-no," Paige stammered.

Hollis noticed her slender frame quivered with tension, or was it fear? How on earth was he going to get her to trust him enough to open up to him? "Ah, keeping me in suspense." With a dejected sigh, he released the rail and stepped away from her, every nerve in his body clamoring with dissatisfaction. "Just remember I don't do windows."

She arched her eyebrows. "Am I that transparent?"

"Yes," he said bluntly. "You look like you could use a friend, but I can understand why you wouldn't want to unload on the gardener or a strictly platonic neighbor either."

For a moment she seemed shocked by his bluntness. Then she smiled, her fingers settling on his chest over the bandage covering the incision where the tube was removed from his lung. "I'll keep the offer in mind, Matt. Something is bothering me. But I'm not ready to talk about it with anyone...not even with a very persuasive nosy neighbor who's agreed to keep the favors between us strictly platonic."

"I didn't kiss you," Hollis said defensively.

"I wouldn't have let you," she retorted in a no-nonsense tone that reminded Hollis of his Aunt Evelyn. "But thanks for caring. Now, come on, the garden is waiting and I'm afraid to pull any weeds without a second opinion."

She scampered down the wrought iron steps in her bare feet. Hollis cleared his throat and glanced down

at her toes. Toes that he'd suckled and savored like
a rare delicacy—and felt a proprietary interest in protecting.

Those steps had to be searing in this heat, not to
mention the asphalt driveway. "Uh, Paige?"

She stopped and whirled around. "Yes?"

"Did you want to put something on your feet?"

"Oh!" The moment she looked down, she started
hopping from one foot to the other and dashed back
up the stairs.

Her face was redder than Audrey's prize roses as
she called over her shoulder, "I forgot to put my
sandals on. I'll be right back."

Hollis stared at her in confusion. Paige definitely
had a lot on her mind. One way or another he was
going to be a party to her thoughts, kisses or no
kisses.

HOLLIS LAY IN BED listening to thunder grate and roll
in the sky overhead like dump trucks colliding into
brick walls. A flash of lightning streaked the sky.
They didn't have storms like this in Vancouver. The
savage display of weather suited his mood. Hollis felt
like growling. It was 1:27 in the morning and he
couldn't sleep. He kept going over every word he and
Paige had exchanged this evening. At least she'd admitted something was bothering her—even if she
wouldn't tell him what.

Another crash of thunder shook the skies, and rum-
bled through the walls of the building. Hollis lifted
his head off the pillow when he heard a muffled
sound. What was that—something being thrown out
a car window onto the street? Or someone backing
into a garbage can?

He lowered his head back onto the pillow and glanced toward the east wall of the bedroom. Paige's bedroom was on the other side of the wall. He'd heard the water run in the pipes and knew she'd probably taken a long cool bath after their picnic supper. The creak of the springs told him when she'd climbed into bed before ten. He'd heard the thunk of a book or a magazine hit the floor half an hour later.

Hollis sighed and tried not to think about how beautiful she'd looked in his bed. How tempting all that golden hair and silken white flesh could be. How seductive her sassing could be. Had she really betrayed him?

She'd looked shaken when he'd suggested taking her to her favorite restaurant, though he'd been careful not to mention it by name.

A shrill cry from next door sent him sitting bolt upright in his bed. His ribs ached from the sudden movement as he scrambled out of bed and pressed his good ear to the common wall between their bedrooms. Was she having nightmares?

"Help!"

The cry was faint but audible, followed by the sound of smashing glass. Hollis's heart leapt to his throat. He didn't know what the hell was going on in there, but he wasn't going back to bed until he knew she was okay. He banged on the wall with his fist and bellowed at the top of his lungs, "Paige? Are you all right? I'm coming over!"

Hollis charged down the narrow stairs in the dark and out his kitchen door in his underwear. His chest burned as he reached Paige's back stoop. To his horror, he found her screen door unlocked, the screen slit. A hole slightly larger than a fist had been made in the decorative glass inset in the exterior door. The door itself was ajar.

"Paige! I'm coming!" Dread knotting his stomach, Hollis stormed the kitchen. Someone tackled him before he had a chance to hit the lights. Hollis flew backward, his back slamming into the refrigerator. Pain jarred his spine, exploded through his ribs and streaked downward to numb his legs.

The hinges on the screen door hissed open, the door closing with a violent clap. Hollis swore at the pain immobilizing his body. Rolling onto his hands and knees, he stretched his arm out to close the interior kitchen door.

His hand connected with something on the floor and sent it skittering away as he lodged his body in front of the door to prevent Paige's attacker from returning. No way in hell was anyone getting through him to get Paige.

"Paige," he called out. "He's gone. Please answer me. I'm down in the kitchen and I'm hurt." Visions of her hurt and bleeding, possibly dying, tortured him.

Why the hell wasn't she answering him?

He ran his palm over the wall above his head, searching for a light switch. Finally, he found the wall plate and the lights flickered on catching Paige hunched on the stairs, her body trembling violently, a baseball bat clenched in her hands. On the floor at the foot of the staircase lay a knife.

Hollis' gaze jerked from the knife to Paige. Her short peach cotton nightie appeared intact. There were no signs of blood or bruising. Relief took the edge off the pain coursing through him. He reached out to her. "It's okay, sweetheart. He's gone. You're safe, but I'm worried I'm not... That's a mean-looking bat you're holding."

"Oh, Matt, thank God it's really you," Paige breathed in a shaky voice, lowering the bat. The shell of strength she projected cracked, leaving a very frightened woman beneath. "I was afraid it was a trick." She hastily descended the last four steps.

"Watch out for the knife—" he warned her.

Paige gave it a wide berth and knelt beside him, concern stamped on her face. She laid the bat on the floor and ran her fingers over him from his head to his shoulders. "Where are you hurt? Did he stab you?" The citrusy scent of her skin and the firm gliding motion of her fingers sent his senses rocketing out of control. A strong stirring in his groin told him he wasn't paralyzed; he'd just had his skeleton rattled. "What's this bandage for?" Paige demanded, indicating the dressing near his left nipple.

"It's nothing. Forget about me," he snapped, clasping her hands before she could explore his body further for injuries. His gray cotton briefs revealed more than he wished. "I'll be fine. What about you? He didn't hurt you, did he?"

"He didn't get the chance. I reached for the baseball bat under my bed the second he eased the door open." She shuddered and Hollis saw the tears well in her eyes and spill down over her pale cheeks. "I was so afraid... Thank God you made such a racket. I think you frightened him." He pulled her roughly against him, threading his fingers into her golden hair as a racking sob escaped from her throat. The feminine feel of her against his chest and thighs caused more soul-deep relief than pain. He couldn't bear to think about what could have happened tonight if he hadn't been here.

"It's okay, it's over now," he murmured. "Did you call the police?"

She stiffened in his arms. "No. Everything happened too fast."

"Well, call now."

She didn't move. Unease tightened his throat when she lowered her gaze. "What's the point?" she mumbled. "I never saw his face or anything. Did you?"

"No, he downed me before I could find the lights. But look, even if you didn't see him, you should still report it. Maybe a rapist has been working this area of the city and they'll be able to get his prints from the knife and prevent him from terrorizing other women."

"Rapist? Oh God, I never thought of that." Her face twisted.

Hollis winced as he tried to stand with her assistance. At least his legs seemed to be working now. With the under cabinet lights on in the kitchen he could see a phone at the end of the counter, but first he leaned over to snag a chair from the table and wedged it under the doorknob just in case. "If you don't want to call the police, I will," he offered.

"No, don't do that!" Paige's eyes were wild with fear.

She clutched at his arm like a frightened child. Hollis swayed under her assault.

Propping his hip against the counter for support, he cupped her head. "It's okay. I know you're afraid but I'll be right by your side the whole time. No one's going to hurt you ever again."

"I said no"

"Then let me call your parents or a friend." Maybe someone she was close to could talk some sense into her. He glanced toward the knife. It wasn't a toy. It could have sliced her to ribbons...

A chill rippled over Hollis's skin. From six feet away, the knife looked sickeningly familiar...the handle exactly the same as the knife his kidnappers had given him to cut himself free. What, had they picked them up at a two-for-one special?

Paige hugged herself tightly, her face stiff and white. "I don't see any reason to upset them needlessly. Nothing happened. But I think I'm going to go away for a few days to get my head together."

Hollis tore his gaze away from the knife as the meaning of her words registered through the suspicions pummeling his mind. Had the kidnappers just tried to eliminate her? Why? Because of her participation in the plot to abduct him? Or because she may have witnessed something at the bombing which could identify them?

He'd been told by the Vancouver police that the C4 bomb placed in the trunk of the car was detonated by a call placed to a cell phone number. To ensure success, the bomber had to have been within viewing distance of the parking lot. One thing was certain, he wasn't going to let her out of his sight until he knew who she was running from and why.

He locked his arms around her. "Paige, you're safe here. I'm not going to let anyone hurt you, I promise. Besides, I'm not going to let you foist the garden off on me."

Paige closed her eyes. She didn't know whether to laugh or to cry or just give in to the heavenly and unwavering warmth of Matt's arms. Her throat ached with the effort of trying to hold back the fear that her assailant tonight had attacked her weeks ago and fathered her baby. She felt so cold she wanted to burrow into the searing heat of Matt's bare skin and stay safe and protected forever, but that wouldn't bring her the answers she needed. She wasn't going to remain here another night like a sitting duck. She'd be better off hunting down her attacker.

"Thank you for helping out tonight, but I'm perfectly capable of taking care of myself for a few days." She shrugged out of the haven of his arms and picked up the baseball bat for emphasis.

"I don't think it's a good idea for you to go off alone—especially after what just happened."

"You don't have any say in the matter."

"The hell I don't." Before Paige knew what was happening, his hands gripped her shoulders and his mouth was descending on hers. His kiss was harsh with emotion and coaxed the protest right out of her until she melted against him, her breasts pressed against the hard wall of his ribs. The baseball bat fell to the floor with a thud as she curled her fingertips into the indentations above his collarbones. Her thumbs nestled in the crisp patch of sandy hair spanning the breadth of his chest. She'd never experienced a kiss that beckoned her with a velvet heat, teasing her, provoking her, promising her an ecstasy beyond all expectation.

A delightful achey sensation tingled from her breasts to the core of her being. With a soft sigh of surrender, Paige rocked her hips against the fullness of Matt's arousal.

He broke their kiss for a moment, his breathing ragged.

"Now do you get it, you stubborn, argumentative woman?" he murmured in her ear, the rasp of his unshaven jaw against the delicate skin of her cheek giving her goose bumps. His fingers stroked her hair. "I've been wanting to kiss you for so long... Did anyone ever tell you that you kiss with as much sugar and spice as you talk?"

Paige wanted to clap her hands over her ears. How could she have allowed him to kiss her? The truth was she didn't *know* if the father of her baby had ever said such nice things to her or made her heart spin out of control when he kissed her. Oh, God, she wanted the father of her baby to be someone sexy like Matt with a good sense of humor—not a man who preyed viciously on women.

She tried to extricate herself from his embrace.

"Matt, I can't—"

"Why not?" he interrupted her, loosening his hold around her. "You just did." He tenderly cupped her chin when she tried to back farther away from him. "And if I'm not mistaken, you enjoyed it as much as I did."

Paige colored and her eyes stung with a fresh batch of tears. Anger at herself and the whole blasted situation cut the last thread of her restraint. Her voice rose sharply. "If you must know, I can't get involved with anyone right now—particularly nearly naked men in their underwear, with bandages on their chest—because I'm pregnant and I don't know who the father is!"

Chapter Five

Pregnant? Hollis shook his head as his heart dropped like an anchor to the pit of his stomach. Surely he hadn't heard right? Sweat dampened his palms. This was not the confession he'd been anticipating. He eyed Paige as if she held a loaded shotgun aimed straight at his heart.

For the first time in his life, the boy who'd been abandoned by his father and deflected endless ridicule at the mouths of his cousins didn't have a snappy comeback.

He felt betrayed and lied to and experienced a hundred other doubts about the perturbing fact she didn't know who the father was. He wanted to throw it all back in her face, hurt her the way she was torturing him. But he didn't. He couldn't. She looked so miserable and unhappy. Her eyes were red, her face was pink and tear-streaked and her beautiful hair was tangled and knotted.

They'd made love twice and both times Hollis had used protection. The chances were slim the baby was his. But Hollis couldn't walk away from the possibility—even if Paige had betrayed him. He knew far too painfully what it felt like to be neglected by a father. His father, a visual artist, had decided the cut-throat Hollis family atmosphere wasn't conducive to creating great art and took off when he was three years old.

Hollis opened his arms to her.

She clung to him sobbing, her tears soaking the dressing taped to his chest. Hollis didn't know how long he held her, but his own eyes were damp with the agony of his suspicions by the time her sobs had subsided. Was it possible she'd been on the rebound and already pregnant when they'd met? Maybe looking for a rich father for her baby? He handed her a paper towel to wipe her face and blow her nose. "Here, I'd give you a tissue, but this is more absorbent."

Her weak snort of laughter made him smile.

"That's better. First things first. Let's check out the downstairs and make sure the intruder didn't help himself to any of your belongings. Then I'll make you a cup of tea and you can tell me all about your pregnancy." He struggled to keep things light. "Though, I'm dreadfully disappointed I'm not the first man you've kissed. At least I hope I'm the first man who's offered to make you tea in the middle of the night."

"Let's just say you're definitely the handsomest man in recent memory who's graced this kitchen in his underwear."

Hollis frowned down at her as he settled his arm around her shoulders. *Just how many men had graced her kitchen in their underwear?* They made a quick tour of the downstairs. His hope that finding she'd been robbed might finally convince her to call the police evaporated when she told him nothing appeared to be missing.

When they returned to the kitchen he ordered her to sit down while he filled the kettle with fresh water, then he rummaged in a drawer for a plastic bag to slip the knife in to preserve any fingerprints that might be on it.

"Why are you doing that?" she asked.

He shot her a pointed glance over his shoulder. "I would think that would be obvious. Don't you ever watch TV? They do this on cop shows all the time."

Color flared in her cheeks. "I meant, what do you plan to do with it?"

"Keep it in a safe place in case you decide to be reasonable and call the police."

"I'm always reasonable."

"That's a matter of opinion." He plopped a tea bag into a teacup he'd found in a cupboard. "Now, stop stalling and start talking about the baby."

That deflated her. She clasped her hands together on the table until her knuckles glowed white. "There's actually not a lot to tell—and what little there is sounds like a movie-of-the-week. I woke up on July fifteenth, well, I didn't know it was July fifteenth at the time, and I felt terrible like I'd come down with the flu. It wasn't until I walked down to the pharmacy to buy aspirin that I realized it wasn't the day I thought it should be—that it was practically six weeks later." She drew a shuddering breath as he passed her a cup of chamomile tea. "Thanks."

Hollis kept a tight rein on his warring feelings as he listened to her tale of finding a bottle of prescription pills in her sundress and the result of her conversation with the emergency ward doctor in Vancouver. "In a way I was relieved to be told about the explosion—it gave me a logical explanation for my memory loss, though the doctor was concerned that I couldn't remember any details as to how I got back to Montreal. My family doctor did some more tests and told me I'd probably recover my memory in time." Her voice wavered. "As far as I'm concerned, it can't happen soon enough. That research trip was very important to me. My best friend's husband, Claude Belanger, was the first victim in the string of kidnappings." Her expressive eyes clouded when she told him about her lifelong friendship with Brenda Thompson. "I'd been in touch with a professor at the University of Ottawa. He's a criminologist who's written papers on the newly evolving field of criminal profiling. After reading Professor Zbarsky's work, I realized that interviewing surviving victims might reveal some behavioral clues about the kidnappers— who they are, how they select their victims, what might be motivating their actions. I'd even planned to talk to as many executives as possible in family-owned companies for their perspective."

Hollis stared at her wanting to believe in the honesty that seemed to ring true in every word, but he hadn't fought his way to the presidency of Pacific Gateway Shipping without being able to detect loopholes—and her story was full of them. Why hadn't she told him in Vancouver that her best friend's husband had been the kidnappers' first victim? Was she merely being a journalist protecting her sources? Or did that simply explain how Claude Belanger was chosen?

Paige toyed with the handle of her teacup. "After I learned I was injured in the same bombing that killed Hollis Fenton, I couldn't help but wonder if I'd spoken to him before he died."

Hollis went completely still at the sound of his name on her lips, but Paige seemed oblivious to him.

"Unfortunately, I lost my briefcase, my files and my laptop computer—I think they were stolen from my car while I was in hospital—so I'll never know what information was given to me or who I was able to contact." She sighed, a frown creasing her brow. "I thought I was experiencing the nausea and the fatigue because I was trying to force my memory, so I stopped trying to do that, which is why I never brought up that second favor I wanted of you. I figured being a headhunter, you might be familiar with some of the family-owned companies and be able to offer a perspective I haven't considered."

The irony of her remark brought a half-hearted grin to his lips. "Ah, one mystery solved. Now when do you get to the part about who fathered your baby?"

She stared down at the table and Hollis felt every muscle in his body clench. She looked ashamed and so unlike the glowing, confident woman who'd knocked the wind from his sails in Vancouver. Unable to stop himself from reaching out to her, he closed his fingers over her hand. Her fingers were icy.

"I went to see my doctor again this morning and she did a pregnancy test. She seems to think I'm five to seven weeks along... It's too soon to do an ultrasound which would be more precise. Apparently I encountered the father of my child during my trip."

Five to seven weeks? Hollis did some rapid mental calculations and tightened his fingers around hers.

He listened as she told him about the research

she'd done on amnesia and her fear that the reason she couldn't remember waking up in the hospital or anything about her return drive home was because something horrible had happened to her during the trip that her mind had chosen to repress rather than deal with.

"It's strange…when I woke up that first day I was so relieved to be home safe. I remembered thinking something similar when I stayed overnight in the hospital. I wondered if maybe my subconscious wasn't trying to tell me something. It seems very possible to me that the person who tried to attack me tonight had attacked me once before. I think he knew where to find me because he'd stolen my briefcase and my computer."

Guilt, anger and a desire to kill whoever had hurt her caught Hollis in a stranglehold. If he hadn't listened to the police's suspicions, Paige wouldn't have driven across the country—alone and vulnerable.

"All the more reason to call the police and let them investigate," Hollis said rigidly.

"Investigate what…a crime the victim doesn't remember? I don't even have the dress. I got rid of it. Besides, I'm tired of hiding out in my own home waiting for my memory to return and I'm certainly not going to wait around another couple of weeks for my first appointment with the psychiatrist—or for the ultrasound to tell me how far along I am. I'll get answers a lot sooner if I try to retrace my trip home. If I'm lucky something will stimulate my memory or I'll track down my computer and my files."

Hollis wanted to put an immediate halt to her dangerous scheme by telling her that her baby was conceived during the most intensely fulfilling night of his life in the bedroom of his False Creek condo, but maybe that was just wishful thinking. He was far too aware that his feelings for Paige could be coloring his perception of the kind of person she truly was. The clues to Christine's condition had been there in front of him, but by the time he'd noticed it was too late.

He cleared his throat, feeling self-conscious and awkward. "How do you know the baby wasn't the result of a one-night stand with a guy you met in a restaurant or in a bar?"

Her silver eyes pierced him, hot with indignation. "I don't. But since I'm not in the habit of sleeping with men I barely know, it's a safe bet for me to assume that I either cared enough about the man for our relationship to reach that stage or someone took advantage of me. And just for the record, my old-fashioned values won't let me become intimately involved with anyone else until I know for certain who fathered my baby."

Hollis didn't mind being put in his place one bit, but he'd obviously made her mad. He quickly changed the subject. "So, how do you propose to go about retracing your trip?"

"Through a combination of educated guesswork and my expense receipts. Fortunately habit served me well and I automatically stuffed all my receipts in my wallet."

He shifted in his chair. "I don't suppose there would be anything I could say or do to talk you out of this? You could be heading straight into more trouble."

She shook her head, her chin jutting up in a stubborn angle. "That's a chance I'm willing to take. I've put my life on hold long enough. I need to do something proactive or I'll go nuts."

"How would you feel about some company, then? You're obviously proficient with a baseball bat, but maybe two heads would be better than one."

Paige wondered if she'd heard correctly. Her pulse quickened, thrumming unsteadily in the hollow at the base of her throat. Maybe he was offering out of a sense of chivalry. "It's very generous of you, but I couldn't possibly accept. What about the executive search you're working on?"

He shrugged. "One of the advantages of being self-employed is that you have control over your schedule. I'm long overdue for some time off." He ran his index finger over the knuckles of her right hand, his voice lowering persuasively. "Besides, as much as I admire your courage, my old-fashioned values balk at the prospect of you driving off into a potentially dangerous situation. We can hire a gardener to care for Audrey's garden and leave today if you want."

"But this could take two or three weeks...maybe longer," she protested. She knew exactly what kind of dent her illness was putting in her personal income. Her sense of ethics wouldn't let her dream of touching the money her father kept depositing in her savings account. The bankruptcy of his custom tailor shop had wounded his pride. She knew it made him feel good to know he could still provide luxuries for his wife and daughters from his other investment income, but she worried he needed the money more than she did.

"My business isn't going to grind to a halt in two weeks or even a month. My clients understand that it takes time and careful research to find just the right executive to enhance their companies and they pay handsomely for the service. I can afford to play hooky with a lady in distress.''

Paige could have kissed him. Then she remembered she already had, and the fact they'd both obviously enjoyed it—despite her present condition—made her blush ruefully. Not many men would take on a single woman and her problems, but then Matt was proving to her in so many ways that he was singularly different from anyone she could remember meeting. No man had made her knuckles tingle at his touch before.

Her lips twitched. ''Sounds to me like you're looking for the first excuse you can find to bail out on the garden.''

His eyes darkened, heating with a hazel cast in the dim light of her kitchen. ''Interpret it however you want. I'm coming with you.''

''I'm not objecting. I've always liked the company of Boy Scouts.'' Besides, baseball bat or no, she felt a lot braver about facing the unknown with a friend at her side—particularly one who looked as physically intimidating as Matt. She had to think about the baby's safety, too.

To her surprise he glowered at her. ''For the record, I was never a Boy Scout.''

Paige laughed. ''My mistake. Sensitive, aren't you?''

''Well, before you leap to any other conclusions about my character I'll get dressed and call someone to fix this window. We'll get a locksmith over here in the morning to put a decent key-operated dead bolt lock in this door and check out the other locks to discourage your visitor from making a return call.''

Paige rose from the table. ''I can call. I'm not helpless—''

''I never implied you were. But wouldn't your time be better spent arranging those receipts you told me about? If we're hitting the road sometime today, we'll need an itinerary.''

''Oh.'' She folded her arms across her chest. ''You know, you're irritating when you're right.''

''It's part of my charm. Are you going to be okay here for a few minutes by yourself?''

''Of course. Just leave the bat.''

Paige bit back a wistful sigh as he fetched the bat and leaned it against the edge of the table with a crooked smile that did funny things to her insides. She couldn't put her finger on it, but he seemed different somehow. Maybe she was seeing him in a different light because she'd unveiled her secrets and he hadn't turned his back on her. Or maybe it was all that exposed male flesh.

An oppressive silence descended upon her little kitchen, thick with the awareness of how very narrow her escape had been from her attacker. A long, slow shudder worked its way up her body, crimping her spine. Paige gripped the end of the bat and hefted it over her shoulder to ward off the unanswered questions that seemed to whisper at her from the shadowy corners of the room. With a backward glance toward the broken pane in her kitchen door, she marched down the hall to her office to gather her receipts and her file on the kidnapping. As far as she was concerned, they couldn't leave soon enough.

HOLLIS STARED AT THE familiar hazel eyes gazing back at him in the mirror and cursed his stupidity as he reached for the plastic case his disposable contact lenses were soaking in. Had Paige noticed that his eyes had suddenly changed color?

She hadn't said anything, but then, maybe she already knew damn well who he was and this little trip would lead him straight to a shallow grave on the side of a lonely road. Driving off to God knew where with a woman he was trusting on the basis of a week's acquaintance didn't seem like the most brilliant plan Hollis had ever come up with. But then, his options were somewhat limited at the moment.

The possibility that Paige might be carrying his child had knocked him clear out of the ballpark and into the stratosphere, while the fear that she'd been raped burned a hole the size of the planet in his stomach. It was ironic that part of his initial attraction to Paige had been the fresh glow of candor that embraced her personality. Now his whole life depended on whether or not she was telling the truth. Hollis tried to insert the colored blue lenses, but his arm trembled so much it took longer than it should.

Then he changed the sodden dressing on his chest for a fresh one and moved into Audrey's bedroom where he pulled on a pair of black shorts and a black T-shirt. He glanced at the time as he picked his watch off the bedside table. It was almost 3:00 a.m. He didn't want to leave Paige alone for too long, but he wasn't quitting Montreal without advising Noreen of the situation.

His secretary answered with brisk efficiency on the second ring as if she were still in the office and not roused from her bed at midnight west coast time.

"Oh, Mr. Fenton, I'm glad you've called. I've heard something back from the private investigator—"

"Hold on, Noreen, I don't have much time," he said, getting directly to the point with his usual bluntness. "Paige was attacked an hour and a half ago by someone carrying a knife that looks remarkably like the knife the kidnappers gave me to escape—only this knife was sharp enough to kill."

"Good heavens!" Noreen gasped. "Is she all right?"

"Fortunately, not a scratch. She beat him off with a baseball bat."

"Why would the kidnappers want to kill her?"

Hollis ran his hand over his hair. "I don't know. Maybe she double-crossed them or maybe they consider her amnesia a threat to their operation." He paused. "Or maybe she's an innocent pawn in this and they think she saw something that could identify them so they're taking her out of the picture."

"Sounds to me like you're leaning toward the latter theory," Noreen observed dryly. "Have you been able to convince her to confide in you as you'd hoped?"

Hollis didn't want to open that particular can of worms. "She's told me of her amnesia, which is why I'm calling. God help me, Noreen, she sounded so honest. She's determined to retrace her trip to Vancouver in hopes of stimulating her memory. I've convinced her to let me tag along for protection."

"She didn't by any chance happen to confide the source of some lump sum deposits that have been made to her personal savings account in the last year, did she? The private investigator thought it odd the deposits began shortly after Claude Belanger's kidnapping and were made in three to six week intervals. Plus, they were in increments in the thousands of dollars: three thousand dollars, five thousand dollars, ten thousand dollars.'' Noreen continued to read off the amounts of the individual deposits. ''She's deposited seventy-two thousand dollars so far—and they definitely didn't come from her business account.''

Hollis swore. He had to admit it was suspicious.

''Have the police come up with any new leads?''

''None that they're sharing. Though they're working closely with the police departments in Calgary, Toronto, Winnipeg and Montreal. And they've requested assistance from the Canadian Bomb Data Center—there's lots of speculation the kidnappers have an IRA connection or a connection with a biker gang. Of course, I'm also told anyone with electronics expertise can find out how to build a bomb from the Internet. They have found out when and where the car was stolen from and questioned the owner and people living in the same neighborhood several times in hopes someone saw something. Sergeant Thurlo told your uncle they received a deluge of calls after the Crime Stoppers segment on the car theft and the bombing aired and that they're investigating every call. Apparently there's a possibility the plastics explosives can be traced, as well as the cell phone that triggered the explosion, but they have to assemble all the pieces first.''

''Well, keep on them.'' He gave Noreen the license plate of his rental car. ''I'll touch base with you as often as possible. But if I suddenly drop off the face of the earth, turn over Paige's laptop and her file to the police. I'm keeping my copy of her file with me under lock and key.''

"Please be careful, sir, and hurry back. Your Aunt Evelyn has gone to great pains to assure our clients and the staff that she's taking over the helm of Pacific Gateway Shipping. Your cousin Sandford is backing her all the way. Speculation is running high at the water cooler that Sandford's next in line to take over the Hollis Group when your uncle steps down.''

Sandford was Evelyn's son. But Hollis figured Evelyn's daughter Camille, and Uncle Luther's three sons, Dalton, Nolan and Parker might have something to say about who took over the family empire. Uncle Luther's daughter Isabelle probably thought her husband Jeff Chalmers, who was one of the board of directors, should be in the running, too.

"It's flattering to know my death has cleared the field for the rest of them.'' Hollis hung up the phone with a wry grin. Most of his life he'd hated his family and their backstabbing ways, but now he realized that dealing with their constant shenanigans had trained him well to deal with any situation Paige threw at him—even a baby.

OTTAWA WAS THEIR first destination and an interview with Professor Zbarsky, the criminologist at the University of Ottawa whom Paige had consulted about the kidnappings. Paige clutched the legal pad in her lap that contained the itinerary she'd been slaving over since early this morning as Matt's metal-gray Lexus joined the throng of cars weaving across the Jacques Cartier bridge, leaving Montreal's sophisticated cityscape of modern glass juxtaposed amongst ancient stone shimmering behind them in a haze of heat.

She bit down on her lower lip and shot a worried glance at Matt's rugged profile. From the moment she'd climbed into his car, she'd been distinctly aware of his presence beside her and the scent of his sandalwood aftershave mingling with the rich leather aroma of the car's interior.

The dark sunglasses concealing his eyes prevented her from telling if he was regretting his generous offer to help her out. He'd done so much already. Between overseeing the window replacement and ensuring her locks were the best possible, he'd helped her piece together a sketchy itinerary poring over her receipts and a list of people she'd hoped to interview, including the kidnapping victims. She also let him read the new file she'd been compiling about the kidnappings. The man absorbed details like a sponge. "I'd still feel better if we took my car," she blurted out.

"That's easy for you to say—you're not six foot one. That car you drive is made for fun, not comfort on cross-country treks. Besides, your attacker might recognize your car and we wouldn't want to give him an advantage." He reached over, his fingers brushing her knee for an instant.

Paige's thoughts scattered with the sensations rioting in her kneecap. "I know it makes sense. I'm just used to being independent."

"No kidding, I hadn't noticed. And I'm sure the locksmith didn't either when you insisted he hand me back the cash I'd given him so you could flash your credit card. You could simply have paid me back."

The dry amusement in his tone rippled through her, loosening the tension knotting her nerves.

The thought that he was very good for her unfolded deliciously in Paige's mind like a note bearing a secret message. She smiled, leaning back against the headrest. "I was setting a standard; it was the principle of the thing. Which reminds me, I revealed my darkest secret to you and now it's your turn to give over."

"I beg your pardon?" His sandy brows rose, emphasizing the thin pink scar that arced over his right eyebrow.

"What's the matter, afraid to tell me the story of your life?"

"When you put it that way, I am. What do you want to know?"

"You could start with the bandage I noticed on your chest. How did you hurt yourself?"

"Let me get this straight. Out of all the questions you could ask me like how old was I the first time I slept with a woman…and did I ever commit a crime, you want to know about the bandage on my chest?"

"It seems a fair question. Besides, it'll take us two hours to get to Ottawa—that'll give us plenty of time to cover all those other things. Now stop stalling and start talking."

IN THE INTEREST OF cementing the trust between them, Hollis evaded most of Paige's questions and lied through his teeth. Though he'd valiantly tried to distract her—particularly about the scars on his body, by the time they pulled up outside Professor Zbarsky's house in the Glebe, his back was coated with sweat and his mind felt as if it had been put through

a meat grinder. He'd tried to keep things simple and
told her his male ego would die of humiliation if he
admitted how he'd gotten hurt, but Paige pressed him
until he finally confessed he'd fallen through a plate
glass window while learning how to in-line skate.
Then she moved on to his personal life, questioning
every kernel of information he reluctantly gave her.
The worst part of it was he'd somehow given her the
impression that he was not only divorced, but that
he'd fallen out of love with Christine.

That misrepresentation irked him the most.

Christine had deceived him and he'd threatened
her with divorce to get her to take her medication,
but he hadn't fallen out of love with her. And he
wouldn't have abandoned her because she was sick.
His marriage vows had meant too much to him. But
he'd regret to his dying day that he'd failed her when
she needed him the most—that she'd killed herself
because she'd interpreted his threat to mean their
marriage was over.

The smell of freshly-mown grass drifted in the
early evening air when Hollis climbed out of the car
and stretched his legs. Paige looked pale, her eyes
sharp and determined, when he came round to open
her door for her. This time she didn't even berate
him for the courteous gesture as she'd done when
they'd stopped at a rest stop forty minutes ago so she
could use the facilities. Hollis hoped she'd take it
easier on Professor Zbarsky than she had on him as
they walked up a flagstone path to a plain yellow
brick house shaded by two towering blue spruces.

No one answered the doorbell, but the faint drone
of a lawn mower suggested someone might be in the
rear yard. They followed a cedar-mulch path past a

bed of feathery pink-tipped astilbe to a brown picket gate on the side of the house. A tanned, robust gentleman, in his mid to late fifties, with a grizzly iron-gray beard and a wide-brimmed straw hat was mowing the lawn in his bathing suit. Slivers of grass clung to his navy canvas shoes.

He cut the engine on the mower when he noticed them.

Somewhere between the car and the backyard Paige had found the confidence Hollis had encountered in Vancouver. She stepped forward with a smile, her hand outstretched. "Professor Zbarsky? I'm Paige Roberts."

A flicker of surprise and curiosity registered on Zbarsky's deeply tanned face. He took her hand. "Yes, of course, Ms. Roberts. I thought I might be hearing from you again."

"I apologize for dropping in without calling first, but the circumstances are a little extraordinary."

Professor Zbarsky nodded. "I see. You've found out more information about the kidnappings, I gather." He gestured toward the screen porch. "Please, make yourselves comfortable while I make myself presentable, then you can introduce me to your companion and we can talk. Your timing couldn't be better...another day and I'd be at my cottage in Chelsea."

Hollis sat on a cushioned lounger across from Paige.

When Zbarsky returned, the hat was gone and he had put on a fresh white undershirt. He carried a tray bearing three glasses of iced tea, a manila file folder, a steno notebook and a silver pen.

Hollis had to hand it to the professor as Paige made

introductions and explained about her amnesia. Zbarsky had probably heard so many outlandish and improbable stories from students, nothing fazed him anymore.

Zbarsky nodded as if he understood completely and reached for the file folder. ''Let me reassure you, Ms. Roberts, I remember our conversation well. We were comparing the differences and the similarities of the kidnappings with the objective of developing a profile about the kidnappers. I admit I have been thinking a great deal about our discussion since the latest kidnapping—even doing some research. My students will have an interesting sample case scenario to analyze next term.''

Great, Hollis thought. His life was a sample case scenario for criminology students.

''What do you think of the fact that Hollis Fenton was abducted on a Saturday when the banks are only open for a limited time?'' Paige asked. ''It seems inconsistent with the modus operandi of the other kidnappings. I would think the longer they held him, the more risk they assumed.''

''It may or may not be significant,'' Zbarsky speculated. ''Fenton may have been most vulnerable that day—a lone man in an isolated area. Or the kidnappers were varying their routine to keep the police at bay…just as they varied how the families were notified of the location of the victim's release to ensure the media made it known that if the families paid the ransom and did not contact the police, they would get their loved one safely home. Make no mistake, I believe they murdered Fenton for the sole purpose of establishing their absolute power and control over the situation—and over every family-owned corporation in the country. Each kidnapping is deliberate and calculated to help them achieve their goals.''

Hollis noticed Paige had turned to a blank sheet on the legal pad and had pulled a pen from her purse to jot down notes.

The professor glanced down at a photocopy of a newspaper article in his file. Sections of the article were highlighted in yellow marker. ''Look at their choice of a first victim. Belanger was young, handsome, successful and perhaps most importantly, he had a wife and a baby. He and his wife were both from wealthy families with resources. He was president of an international translation and document management company. Their every instinct would be to draw upon those vast resources, fight back, get the police involved. The kidnappers didn't touch the money. Instead, they boldly called the police and told them their involvement had signed Belanger's death certificate. The country was outraged and the media plastered Belanger's face and the details of his murder on papers across the country.''

''Along with the subtle message that if the family had played by the rules, the husband and father would have been returned to them unharmed,'' Paige added.

''Precisely. You will note the second abduction took place two months later before the memory of Belanger's death could fade from the public eye. They chose a woman from Winnipeg, Susan Platham-Burke. An only child. She was engaged, but no children. Though she didn't hold the office of president like the other victims, she was the director of public relations—an extremely attractive blonde, who was well known and respected for her involvement in children's charities in the area. The family heeded the kidnappers' warning and didn't contact the police. The ransom was paid and she was returned unharmed. The family managed to keep the news of her abduction under wraps for almost a month before the story broke." Zbarsky paused. "I think it was the family's success at nearly keeping a lid on the story that provoked the kidnappers into calling the local paper to advise them of the release location of the third victim, Will Harper, in Calgary four months later. Calling the newspaper ensured that the country knew another kidnapping had occurred and that the victim was returned because the family had obeyed the kidnappers' instructions to the letter. It wasn't a coincidence that Harper was abducted a week before Christmas. His wife was expecting their first child."

Zbarsky indicated another article bearing a photo of a thirty-something brunette with an engaging smile. "Ellen Cummings, a mother of five in Halifax, had narrowly survived a bad car accident the year before and needed the services of her own home health care company. The kidnappers called a local television station. They're selecting their victims for maximum emotional impact on the media and the families involved."

Hollis frowned. In no way, shape or form could he see his abduction as having a substantial emotional impact on his family or the public-at-large. Though, he supposed he should be grateful his Uncle Luther had coughed up the 1.5 million. "What was Fenton's appeal?" he asked out loud. "The articles Paige showed me said he was single—or widowed actually. Sure the Canada Day weekend is a patriotic holiday, but it doesn't exactly compare with Christmas."

"No, but it was a brilliant means of emphasizing the threat posed to all *Canadian* executives." Paige thoughtfully tapped her pen on her notepad. "There weren't any pictures of Fenton in the articles I read, but the fact that he is described as being very attractive suggests he was a photogenic symbol—like all the other victims."

"Very good Ms. Roberts," Professor Zbarsky said. "I suspect the police had a hand in keeping Fenton's photo out of papers. I couldn't find one in the sources I checked, either." He lifted a finger to make a point. "Remember, all behavior is purposive. By contacting the media in the Harper and Cummings kidnappings, the kidnappers exhibited a need to have their crimes publicized. An RCMP profiler or a psychologist called in to consult on the investigation of the kidnappings probably suggested that the police thwart the kidnappers' need for publicity by depriving them of the human face they want attached to their actions."

"It still seems odd to me that they would choose him," Hollis persisted. "He had all those cousins. It would be more logical for the kidnappers to abduct one of Luther Hollis's children who took a good picture."

Zbarsky nodded. "The same question occurred to me. Luther Hollis is a legendary figure in Western Canada. He took over his father's empire when he was thirty and tripled its net worth in ten years. He's still making money hand over fist. The research I've gathered on the Hollis family on the Internet suggests that Fenton was the purported heir to Luther Hollis's throne. In effect, they abducted the crown prince."

Hollis's heart felt as cold as the glass of tea he held in his hand.

"If the kidnappers' objective is to hold Canadian corporations hostage and to use the media to achieve that end, why didn't they contact the media directly to apprise them of Fenton's release location like they did with Harper and Cummings?" Paige asked.

"They did one step better," Zbarsky replied. "They contacted his family, but they didn't name his release location and thus began a widespread public search for Fenton."

Actually they contacted his secretary Noreen at her home, Hollis thought, which raised an interesting question as to how the kidnappers had found out her unlisted phone number. Of course, he and Paige had spent enough time together that she could have taken it off the speed dial on his home phone. The suspicion rankled. He wondered if any of the other victims had had a new acquaintance drop into their lives just prior to their kidnapping.

Paige's voice broke into his thoughts. "It also upped the drama for the family to think Fenton was tied up and helpless to the elements. It's a shame I can't remember if I spoke to him—or if I was able to interview any of the other victims. It might help us compile a profile of each of the kidnappers."

It might also reveal what the victims had told the police about their kidnappings, Hollis thought cynically. What better way for the kidnappers to keep several steps ahead of the law than to have a legitimate journalist ask questions for them? But why would Paige be involved in such a thing?

The professor gathered his research into a pile. "As I told you at our last meeting, Ms. Roberts, I will be pleased to pursue this matter further if you succeed in being granted interviews with the victims. The planning and resourcefulness necessary to accomplish these crimes suggests the kidnappers are intelligent and knowledgeable about the business world. But I might be able to draw other conclusions from the victims' statements about their ordeals. I will need to know what the abductors did to the victims and exactly what was said. Their actions and their words can provide a barrage of clues, from their attitude to their social class. Now, come into my office and I will make you copies of the materials you originally gave me.''

While Paige followed Zbarsky into the house, Hollis stared out at the dusky shadows deepening in the thick cluster of trees skirting the fringe of the yard. The loss of a night's sleep and the long drive to Ottawa were taking their toll on his body. His ribs ached and the bruised muscles in his back made every movement painful. His new contacts felt uncomfortably dry. Something moved near the base of a tree. He blinked. A quiver of unease brushed the base of his neck as he stared hard at the spot. A moment later, a calico cat emerged from the lower branches of the evergreen and darted across the lawn.

Hollis's heartbeat returned to normal. Paige's attack last night was making him paranoid. He was determined that somehow he and Paige would contrive to speak to the other victims. Paige's meeting with Professor Zbarsky had shown him that more precise and invaluable information might be gained about the kidnappers if the victims personally compared notes of their ordeals rather than relying on the police investigation to piece together information.

Their assumptions could be as misleading as Paige and Professor Zbarsky's assumption that the kidnappers had called his family to notify them of his release.

Hollis was willing to do whatever it took to settle the score with the bastards who'd played God with his life. But it would help a lot if he knew which team Paige was playing on. The most damaging piece of evidence he had against her—aside from the mysterious deposits in her bank account—was a cryptic modus operandi list he'd found in her briefcase. It had contained information about the kidnappings that had never been made public. Was the list merely a compilation of notes she'd taken during interviews with the victims?

At the sound of her laughter, Hollis turned and saw Paige and Zbarsky through the wide patio screen door of the house. They were standing over Zbarsky's kitchen table, which was piled high with books and papers, reminding Hollis of his first glimpse of Paige's desk. The muted yellow light of the amber glass fixture above their heads turned Paige's hair to molten gold. The sight of her smiling and looking more relaxed than he'd seen her in days twisted him inside out.

As they said their goodbyes Zbarsky handed Paige his card, with the phone number at his cottage written on it.

"So, what did you think?" Hollis asked when they reached the privacy of his car. "Did it stir any memories?"

"Not a one." Paige sighed. "Professor Zbarsky's theories make a lot of sense. Though I have a strong gut feeling that Fenton was picked in lieu of his cousins because he was disposable.''

Hollis's fingers tightened around the key as he slid it into the ignition. ''How so?''

''Maybe the kidnappers expected Luther Hollis might not play by their rules.''

''He obviously didn't.''

''Exactly. Hollis Fenton could have been an example for anyone else who thought they were arrogant enough to cross the kidnappers, which suggests they have other targets in mind.''

''You'd think the money the kidnappers had collected would be enough. Why not quit while they're ahead, after four successful ransom deliveries?'' The 1.5 million the kidnappers had received after his abduction should have kept them afloat for a considerable amount of time.

''Don't count on it. We don't know what the money's being used for. It could be divvied up among the members for their personal use or be going to fund a specific cause. It's possible the kidnappings aren't even motivated by money. There may be a grudge involved and the money is secondary.''

''God help the families of the next victims.'' Hollis pressed his lips into a grim line as he started the Lexus and pulled away from the curb.

THE CRIMINOLOGIST WAS TOO perceptive to be allowed to live. He made it surprisingly easy. Not half an hour after his visitors had gone, the old guy remembered the lawnmower left out in the yard.

It was child's play to lie in wait for him in the shed nestled in the back corner of the property with a sledgehammer found in the open tool locker. The old guy didn't even see the blow coming.

It took less than ten minutes to empty the tools from the airtight durable plastic locker and stuff Zbarsky's body inside. Then he closed the door of the shed and put the padlock in place.

Gathering up the file about the kidnappings and finding the professor's car keys took longer. With the lights out and the doors locked, nobody would be looking for the old man for a good long time.

Now Paige Roberts was the only loose end.

The killer drove the old guy's car up to Bank Street and found a place to pull over to make the call. Calmly, efficiently, a number was entered into the cell phone. "The job's done," he said to the answering voice. "It's your turn."

Chapter Six

Paige never expected pregnancy to be such a physical and emotional roller coaster. When Brenda was pregnant with Alexandre, she'd glowed with such radiance that complete strangers stopped her in the street and patted her stomach. She'd eaten with relish anything that even remotely resembled food. And optimism for the future rang in her every sentence. She'd made impending motherhood enviable.

Paige's circumstances were anything but enviable. She looked ghastly not glowing, when she checked her face in the ladies' room mirror of the Italian restaurant where they'd stopped for dinner on their way to downtown Ottawa. Lipstick wouldn't help so she left it off and splashed cold water on her face. At least she felt semioptimistic after her interview with Professor Zbarsky. It had gone much better than she'd expected. And her stomach hadn't vetoed the menu's vast selection of pasta and salad.

As Paige dried her face with a paper towel, she remembered she'd left the automobile club book with the hotel listings in Matt's car. They'd have to find a place to stay tonight, and it would be easier on her stomach to study the map in the restaurant than in a moving car.

She made her way back to the table, feeling her heart lift on invisible wings when her eyes met Matt's clear blue ones across the restaurant.

He was finishing the lasagna and the beer he'd ordered.

"You okay?" he asked, rising as she approached.

"I'm fine," she said far too brightly, gripping the back of her chair to prevent him from pulling it out for her. "Mind if I borrow the keys to your car? I forgot something—"

"Tell me what it is and I'll get it for you."

"You've already done enough for me today. Enjoy the rest of your dinner."

"I insist," he said with such a deep-throated growl that Paige almost felt compelled to give in. But that would mean she'd have to confess that reading in the car made her queasy.

"Matt, I'm pregnant, not helpless."

He dug the keys out of the pocket of his tan slacks with obvious reluctance. "You forgot stubborn and independent."

She grinned at him. "I believe we've already agreed on that issue."

The keys were warm from the heat of his body. She jiggled them in her fingers and hummed an old song about heroes under her breath as she exited the restaurant and walked to the crosswalk at the corner. Matt's car was parked on the opposite side of the street, almost directly across from the restaurant, but Paige was too law-abiding by nature to jaywalk.

Unfortunately, the driver in the southbound lane who streaked through the red light and swerved toward her with a squealing of tires was not so law-abiding. And probably drunk, too.

HOLLIS WANTED TO TRUST her. As Paige walked away from him, her purse in one hand, the keys to his rental car in the other, every cell in his heart urged him to keep his butt firmly planted in his chair. She'd come back. His mind, on the other hand, cynical as always, told him to quit wasting time and get outside where he could catch her in the act of trying to run off with his car.

His cynical side won. When he didn't spot her immediately at the Lexus, he worried she'd removed her things from the trunk and disappeared on foot...or hopped into a taxi she'd called when she'd gone to the ladies' room.

Then he spied her, her dark blue skirt and blouse making her almost invisible in the dark as she descended the curb and entered the crosswalk.

He also noticed the blur of a sedan as it passed in front of the restaurant at top speed and approached the stoplight at the intersection without tapping on the brakes. The car seemed to be on a collision course with Paige.

Hollis felt his soul crumple in horror as he darted out into the street after her. Oh, God, it couldn't end like this...

PAIGE REACTED INSTINCTIVELY. There was no time to think. She took two desperate running steps forward and launched herself toward the far curb to save herself and the baby. The sensation of flying was oddly familiar. A scream tore from her throat, "Hollis!"

Her body jarred as she hit the asphalt. The abraded surface tore into her fingers, her forearms, her stomach and her thighs. Pain seared the length of her arms as if someone had put a match to her fingertips.

The car roared off and Paige curled into a protective ball, cradling her stomach. *Please God, let my baby be okay!* she prayed fervently.

She felt strong arms lifting her and opened her eyes to see Matt holding her, anguish stamped on his lean face. "The baby..." she whispered, unable to hide her fear.

"I'll get you to a hospital. The baby will be fine."

Paige was determined to believe him.

HE'D COME SO CLOSE to losing her forever. Hollis insisted they share a room when they checked into the hotel after their trip to the emergency room. Paige didn't argue with him about it as they took the elevator up to the fifth floor. She moved carefully under her own steam, only allowing him to cup her left elbow. Her scrapes had been cleaned up and dressed at the hospital and the doctor had assured her there was no sign the baby was in danger. Hollis cursed himself that the driver of the car had gotten away. It had happened so fast he hadn't thought to get a license plate number, nor had any of the other witnesses.

Paige headed straight for the bathroom as soon as they entered the room. Hollis barged in after her when he heard the sound of her retching.

She was down on her one knee that still had skin on it, leaning over the toilet bowl. "Can't a girl have any privacy?" she demanded, glaring up at him.

Hollis felt a muscle twitch in his jaw as he took a

washcloth from the towel bar and wet it. Then he passed it to her. "Sometimes even stubborn and independent people need help. It's not a sign of weakness. It can be their greatest strength."

"And just what do you get out of it?" she asked, wiping her mouth.

"The pleasure of your charming company."

Paige rolled her eyes and Matt was relieved to see her spunk was rebounding. "You have a twisted definition of charming."

"I hope you're not questioning my judgment. I make a living gauging the merits of individuals and their worth. You've got potential."

She gestured for him to help her stand, her golden hair falling in disarray around her pinched face. "I'm sure the baby will be reassured to hear that." Her silver eyes were wide and deeply troubled as she leaned into him.

Hollis's throat tightened at the light pressure of her hand on his forearm. He was painfully aware that but for the grace of God, Paige would be spending the night in the morgue rather than in a hotel room with him. He curled his other arm protectively around her, fighting the urge to pull her closer when she swayed unsteadily. "Come on. You should be resting."

She moved slowly, dropping the washcloth on the counter. "Matt?"

"Yes?" he murmured, far too aware of how fragile she felt. And how her familiar scent wove through the crevices of his distrust.

"There's something I haven't told you."

Hollis forced his legs to keep moving as she navigated toward the queen size bed nearest the bathroom. He kept his tone noncommittal. "And a near brush with death is putting you in the mood to confess?''

She colored. ''I think I've remembered something. It's not much…maybe it isn't even a memory. I'm not sure. All I know is that when I jumped out of the path of the car, I remembered flying through the air and being hurt.''

He gripped her wrist as they reached the bed. ''Is that all? Think carefully. Do you remember anything else? Sights? Sounds? People?''

Her forehead crinkled into a frown. ''Only one thing. I said *his* name.''

''Whose name?''

''Hollis Fenton's.''

Hollis's gut clenched. He peered at her closely, searching for signs of deception. All he saw was exhaustion and fear mirrored in her eyes.

''Wh-what do you think it means?'' she asked.

A half-dozen possibilities crossed his mind, not all of them positive. He let go of her wrist and turned down the covers on the bed for her, struggling to control the emotions churning beneath his thoughts. ''Maybe you just called out his name because you were trying to attract his attention—to ask him for an interview before the car exploded.'' *Then again, maybe she was remembering him. Might remember them. Might remember if the baby she was carrying was theirs.*

''I suppose that makes sense.''

He laid her suitcase on the bed beside her so she wouldn't have to move.

But Paige didn't open the suitcase or demand privacy so she could change. Hollis gently touched her chin with his finger, wondering where her thoughts were leading her. "Let's hope it means your memory is returning. The accident tonight may have been a coincidence, but I'm not willing to take any chances…so get used to the idea that I'm not letting you out of my sight until your memory returns."

He thought she'd balk at his ultimatum and accuse him of acting like his primeval ancestors. Instead, she smiled at him, a sweet smile of surrender that undermined the thousand and one doubts he had about her.

She clasped his finger and squeezed. "Thanks for being here for me and the baby. You're a good man."

Her touch was platonic, but Hollis felt the intimacy of it pulse through every cell of his being. With a strained smile, he stepped back quickly and muttered something about needing to take a shower.

When he emerged from the shower fifteen minutes later, a towel wrapped around his waist, Paige was asleep in her bed, the sheets pulled up close under her chin. The clothes she'd been wearing were lumped in a teetering pile on top of her suitcase as if she'd been too tired to deal with them.

Hollis turned out the bedside lamp and pulled on a T-shirt and briefs in the dark. Then he slid beneath the covers of the other bed and stared at the silhouette of her body in the bed across from him, wondering if she'd still thank him when her memory returned.

BEING CONFINED IN A car and sharing a room with Matt three nights in a row had subtly changed things between them. From the moment he'd landed on her doorstep, Paige had been aware of the physical impact he had on her senses. But ever since he'd rushed her to the hospital in Ottawa, a layer of familiarity had materialized between them, making it so much harder for her to maintain her distance from him.

The truth was, she needed him. Admitting that fact to herself hadn't been nearly so scary when she'd realized that Matt could so precisely pinpoint her moods because they each possessed an ability to let the world fall by the wayside when they were focused on an important task. Paige glanced up from the street map of Winnipeg she was studying and glanced at Matt's fierce, lean profile, grateful she was his current task at hand, the challenge of the moment. She'd never forget the kiss he gave her the night he'd rescued her from her attacker, but she didn't have any false misconceptions that they'd be anything more than friends. Not with a baby of unknown paternity on the way.

She felt better this morning, less stiff from the accident, though she had some nasty scabs on the underside of her forearms and her left knee. She'd chosen to wear an apricot silk jacket over an amber print dress with a long flared skirt to cover her injuries. Paige noticed that despite her loss of appetite, the dress felt noticeably snug across her breasts.

Since leaving Ottawa, they hadn't been able to keep the same frenetic pace she'd made across the country because of their efforts to stop and ask questions at the food, gas and rest stops Paige had previously made. So far, no one had recognized her or offered information that might indicate she'd met someone or been attacked.

They'd arrived in Winnipeg late last night and had even asked for the same room she'd stayed in a little over a month ago. This morning, they'd eaten in the same coffee shop where Paige had eaten on her previous trip and spoke to the same waitress who'd served her. Paige couldn't blame the people they questioned for not remembering her, but she kept hoping something would at least seem familiar...or even that her subconscious might send her a warning signal.

But there was nothing.

Paige tried to concentrate on their eleven-thirty interview with Susan Platham-Burke—the kidnappers second victim who lived in this city. She'd called Susan Platham-Burke from a pay phone in the coffee shop. She'd had a devil of a time convincing her to give them a few moments of her time. The woman was obviously scared, but once Paige had told her she'd lost her memory in the blast which killed Hollis Fenton, she reluctantly acknowledged that Paige had interviewed her several weeks ago and agreed to meet with them.

They arrived early for their appointment. There was visible security in the lobby of the corporate offices of the Platham-Burke agricultural products empire. A uniformed guard examined their ID, then made a phone call and allowed them access to an elevator to take them to the third floor. Miss Platham-Burke's receptionist asked to examine their identification, as well, then directed them to follow her.

Miss Platham-Burke was not alone in her office. Two gargantuan men with physiques and expressions that suggested they'd graduated with top honors from a mercenary training school, flanked her desk. The glowering distrust in their eyes rattled Paige. It was like standing in front of a pair of unleashed Dobermans.

A petite woman with a short crop of tight blond

curls and compassion hovering in her soft misty blue eyes rose from behind a black lacquered Oriental desk and offered Paige her hand. Her smile was that of a polished socialite, gracious and welcoming, though Paige could feel the tension in the woman's fine-boned fingers. "We meet again, Miss Roberts. Don't mind the boys. They're my fiancé's romantic idea of a prenuptial wedding gift."

Paige gave Miss Platham's-Burke's fingers a squeeze of understanding. "I wish I could say I remember them from our last meeting, but I don't." She gestured at Matt. "This is Matt Darby. He's *my* protection. Thank you for agreeing to see us."

Miss Platham-Burke expelled a shaky breath. "I'm still not sure I'm doing the right thing, so maybe we'd better get this over with before I change my mind. Panicking over the slightest things seems to be a long-term side effect of being kidnapped." A shadow dimmed her eyes. She nervously toyed with the glistening diamond engagement ring on her left hand. "I'm still afraid of it happening again or them seeking some kind of reprisal if we cooperate with the police. But you were generous to share what information you had of Claude Belanger's abduction and my parents and my fiancé are adamant that I not have anything to do with the police investigation— except through a statement we sent via our lawyer. I know they're doing it for my own protection, but I feel I have a responsibility to do whatever I can to prevent this from happening to someone else. All the security and the money in the world won't buy me a restful night until I know the people who did this to me are behind bars."

"That's exactly why I'm here," Paige replied. "I

wanted to share a theory with you about the kidnappings and ask you a few questions about your captors. Maybe I mentioned this theory during our last interview…''

Miss Platham-Burke frowned. ''I don't recall that you mentioned any theories. You interviewed me about my experience and we discussed the similarities between my kidnapping and Mr. Belanger's kidnapping. My heart goes out to his wife and son and their families. I hope you'll pass along my condolences to your friend. Brenda Thompson was her name, wasn't it?''

''Yes.'' Paige was touched Miss Platham-Burke had remembered, but then everything she'd read about the soft-spoken woman suggested she was a sincere humanitarian. Miss Platham-Burke gestured them to join her on a pair of elegant coral silk couches clustered around an Oriental rug in the corner of her office. A black lacquered end table and her desk were crowded with photos of children from all nationalities and income brackets. ''I don't suppose you took notes of our meeting?'' Paige inquired, pulling out her file and a legal pad to take notes. Matt had chosen to sit at the opposite end of the couch, apparently striving to be as unobtrusive to the conversation as Miss Platham-Burke's bodyguards.

''No, I'm sorry. And I asked that you not tape-record our conversation or indicate in any way in your notes that I was the subject of your interview. Have you lost your notes or just can't interpret them?''

Paige flushed. ''They're either misplaced or were stolen from my car along with my computer and my briefcase while I was in hospital...so your precaution was well-advised. I wish I could tell you more.''

Miss Platham-Burke seemed shaken by the loss of the notes. The color drained from her cheeks, but her smile remained in place.

Paige set her notepad aside. ''I won't take notes now either. We'll just talk.'' Slowly, Paige worked her way through Professor Zbarsky's theory as to why each of the victims were selected. She noticed the bodyguards were listening intently, too.

''So you suspect the kidnappers move into an area and then peruse the media looking for potential victims with high-profile appeal?'' Miss Platham-Burke said in a businesslike tone.

Paige nodded. ''Do you keep a media file? An article with an accompanying photo of you might give us an indication of when and how the kidnappers selected you. We might find a common link as to how they operate.''

''Of course I do. I count on publicity to raise awareness of the causes I support. I'll buzz my secretary and ask her to bring in my scrapbooks.'' Miss Platham-Burke rose and used the phone on her desk.

A minute later, a knock sounded on the door and the secretary entered, balancing a pile of leather scrapbooks in her arms. She assured her boss they were up to date as she neatly laid them out on the coffee table. There were eight volumes.

Miss Platham-Burke seemed embarrassed by the pile.

''I keep a separate one for each charity, plus one for company related matters—I'm the public relations officer—and one for personal publicity involving my private life and my family. I employ a clipping service so it should be very thorough. Angela, my secretary, is a whiz at keeping everything in chronological order.''

''You're a researcher's dream,'' Paige declared, opening a scrapbook denoting the name of a children's hospital charity fund. An appealing picture of Miss Platham-Burke with her arm around a giggling young girl in a wheelchair was on the first page. ''Why don't we check each scrapbook for articles which appeared prior to your August kidnapping?''

Matt leaned toward her to peer at the photo. ''You should go back to at least January,'' he murmured discreetly, ''because you don't know how long the kidnappers could have been planning the abductions.''

''We're assuming they picked the cities at random and did their research once they arrived in their selected city,'' Paige hastened to explain. ''But they may have been accessing the articles from newspapers via the Internet or have subscribed to local papers and had their victims selected long before the first abduction occurred.''

Miss Platham-Burke divvied up the albums amongst the three of them. It took an hour to tab the pages for Miss Platham-Burke's secretary to photocopy. Paige realized just how much of an individual's life could be pieced together from the clippings. There were plenty of photos. The secretary brought in a tray of finger sandwiches and a pot of herb tea, then discreetly disappeared to make the copies. ''The articles and the sources they appeared in might even tell us something about the level of education of the kidnappers and their backgrounds,'' Paige remarked, thinking of Professor Zbarsky. She was relieved her stomach found the mint tea soothing. She had a sudden roaring appetite for the egg salad and ham sandwiches.

Miss Platham-Burke appeared pensive. "Do you remember what they said to you? How they spoke?"

"They actually spoke to me as little as possible. Mostly polite commands to please stand up or sit or walk. Their manners were schooled and deferential. My overall impression is that they were well-educated and had corporate working experience. One of them was slick enough to worm my schedule out of Angela by convincing her his company was interested in participating in an event to raise funds for the children's museum. He dropped all the right people's names. Angela wasn't the least bit suspicious. That's how they knew I'd be at the meeting at the restaurant. They'd parked beside my car...they had a hood over my head and a gun pressed to my ribs before I knew what was happening."

"Did you get a glimpse of any of them?"

Miss Platham-Burke shook her head, the tight curls bouncing emphatically. "Unfortunately, no. The meeting finished after nine and it was dark. But I'm certain the car parked beside me was a black minivan. The only thing I can tell you is that I believe there were three of them and one of them may have had gray hair. I had to wear the hood the entire time, but there was a hole cut into it so I could eat. I couldn't see much through the hole except once I glimpsed a gray hair on a blue pant leg when someone came to untie me to deliver me to the drop site. Now whether that meant one of the kidnappers had gray hair or it was a stray hair picked off the upholstery, I don't know. But the kidnappers told me when they shoved me in the van that if I resisted or did anything to remove the hood, they'd have no other recourse but to kill me. Those were their precise words."

Hollis listened intently to the young woman, but her description of her abductors didn't match his impressions. Four men had taken him down. Perhaps one or two of his abductors spoke as if they'd received a university education. But the guy with the cowboy boots had definitely been unrefined in both his language and his manners. He wondered if they'd tried to intimidate him because he was male and had treated Miss Platham-Burke more kindly. Maybe the bastards were sophisticated enough to purposely change their demeanor to prevent the police from developing accurate profiles on them. Maybe one of them had even studied or worked in the law enforcement field.

"They must have been talking to someone close to you if they knew which names to drop," Hollis commented. "Maybe they even got to know you. Do you remember meeting anyone new through any of your committees—a week or two before your abduction? It could have been someone who introduced themselves at a cocktail party...or some other event. Don't presume it could only have been a man." Hollis felt a stabbing thrust of guilt for pressing the point when the "new person" he'd met before his abduction and who'd captured his heart was smiling at him encouragingly. The chilling possibility it could all be an act made him heartsick.

"I meet so many people...no one comes to mind immediately. It was a year ago."

"Do you have any idea where they took you?" Paige asked.

"From the time we spent in the car and the damp smell of the place they took me, I'd guess I was held in a cottage near Lake Winnipeg. The wood floor was painted and it felt uneven. Occasionally I would hear the distant sound of a motorboat. I was tied to a bed for the most part—except when they allowed me to go to the bathroom or sit up to eat. Even then, my feet and one arm were still bound.''

They'd definitely treated her like a lady. Hollis had been tied to a chair. Being hand-fed by his taunting captors had been humiliating experiences. He glanced apologetically at Paige, hoping she wouldn't mind if he intruded again to ask another question or two. "Could you describe the hood? What type of fabric was it made of? Did it seem homemade or commercially manufactured?''

"Mmm, cotton I believe. It was black and loose around my head, definitely not stretchy like Lycra. I'd say it was homemade. I didn't feel a tag sewn into a seam or anything. The hole was roughly cut out with scissors. My lawyer passed the hood along to the police. Frankly, I didn't want to look at it ever again.''

Hollis pressed his lips together. His hood, though homemade, had been fabricated of black velvet. "You said the floor of the cottage was wood. Could you tell if your abductors were wearing hard-soled or soft-soled shoes?''

"Definitely soft soles. Come to think of it, one was heavier than the others, I could always tell he was the one approaching because the floor creaked dramatically.''

So, no hard-heeled cowboy boots. "Were any footprints found by the police at your release location?''

"Not that I'm aware of. But it's doubtful. The police weren't informed of my kidnapping until several weeks after it had occurred. Two of them drove me to Kildonan Park and left me in some decaying leaves. The one I assumed was their leader apologized for hog-tying me and reassured me my family would be there in less than an hour. I don't know where the third person was. My father had delivered the money the night before to a property at the end of a dirt road. He told me it was like something in a movie. He got a call which sent him to a note, which directed him elsewhere to another note. It was sort of like a test to see if he was being followed by the police. He walked out into the woods until someone called out for him to set the knapsack down and leave. My father believed they contacted him from a pay phone all three times because he could always hear traffic noises in the background. He was very careful to do what they said to the letter. He didn't consult anyone but my mother and my fiancé and they all agreed they wouldn't contact the police. We're still not sure how the story leaked to the press. We explained the sudden appearance of the bodyguards by saying it was a precautionary measure after I'd received some threatening letters. My fiancé didn't even tell his own parents."

Hollis met Paige's gaze.

"I think you can blame the kidnappers for the leak," Paige said, voicing his thoughts. "They wanted to show the country that your family had cooperated with their demands and, as a result, they'd gotten their beloved daughter back."

Miss Platham-Burke shuddered and eased back

into the plump cushions of the sofa. "It makes sense in a perverse sort of way."

Paige cleared her throat. "I don't wish to be indelicate, but may I ask what the ransom demand was?"

"It was a million. The same as for Claude Belanger."

Hollis wondered what they'd demanded from Will Harper's and Ellen Cummings's families. They'd obviously gotten greedier in his case—or maybe were trying to make up for lost revenue in Belanger's bungled kidnapping.

The secretary knocked twice and entered, the photocopies tucked in a file that she presented to her boss.

"Your one-thirty appointment has arrived. Shall I ask her to wait a few minutes more?"

Paige felt they'd taken enough of Miss Platham-Burke's time, and a few minutes later took their leave.

Susan Platham-Burke glanced at her bodyguards after her guests had departed. "Did you get the interview on tape?"

"Yes, ma'am."

"Good. I'll be needing several copies." The police had asked her a lot of questions about her first interview with Paige Roberts. Susan was certain they'd find this one doubly interesting. If she had the courage to send it.

SINCE SHE'D GIVEN her word, Paige resisted the urge to write down everything Susan Platham-Burke had shared about her ordeal the instant they returned to the car in the parking lot. Paige decided she'd just have to rely on her faulty memory to store the information.

Susan Platham-Burke's press clippings gave Paige something to peruse as she and Matt headed west on the Trans-Canada Highway. The Manitoba prairie stretched out in flat, and sometimes, undulating, checkerboards of wheat and rye fields, occasionally broken by the appearance of a town or by the low verdant hills hugging the river valleys cutting through the rich farming plains.

Paige read out sections of the articles to Matt and made a list of the sources until she could no longer ignore the blossoming twinges of queasiness starting to flower. She had no idea pregnancy could regulate a woman's every action…her thoughts, her health, her diet, her career, not to mention who she could get involved with. But Paige refused to let her thoughts drift in the direction of her personal relationships—not with Matt so close by.

He'd impressed her during the interview with Susan Platham-Burke, asking questions Paige hadn't thought to ask. She shifted her gaze toward him briefly. His scar peeking out above the dark lenses of his sunglasses made him appear threatening and dangerous. Her bodyguard. Two heads were definitely better than one—she just didn't want to get her heart involved and that seemed more and more difficult to do with each minute they spent together.

Closing the file, she purposefully focused her thoughts away from Matt and made a mental note to ask Brenda about any press Claude had received in the months prior to his kidnapping. During visits to her friend's home, Brenda would sometimes point out articles she'd taped on the refrigerator, but whether or not her friend kept them long-term was another matter.

Paige frowned at the blue sky stretching out endlessly toward the horizon and sighed. Tracking down the kidnappers through the articles was more challenging than finding a diamond stud earring in one of these fields.

"Tired?" Matt asked, reaching over to massage the back of her neck. "I could turn back to Portage La Prairie if you don't think you can make it to Brandon."

She melted under the touch of his fingers, a current of molten heat whisked down her spine and blazed into her belly. They hadn't been on the road more than an hour. Motels were few and far between. Only a dozen towns in the whole province boasted the convenience of accommodations.

"No, I'm not tired. Just frustrated."

"I've got a cure for that." His fingers traced the sensitive spot at the base of her skull. A pleasurable sensation exploded along her scalp.

Paige stared at him wide-eyed with suspicion, her pulse racing like wildfire. He wasn't making it any easier to keep their relationship platonic. "And what would that be?" she dared to ask, jerking her head away from his sensual exploration.

His blunt-tipped fingers dropped to his navy-clad knee. "Blast me."

"I beg your pardon?"

"You know, I start talking, you make a smart comeback and the next thing you know you're loosened up and smiling."

Paige fought back a smile. "You sound as if you enjoy it."

"I do."

"Well, then, you have a peculiar idea of entertainment."

"What's so peculiar about admitting that you enjoy talking to someone? Enjoy seeing them smile." His gaze lingered on her reddening cheeks. "Even blush."

Damn the man. How was she supposed to spend the night with him in a motel room when he said things like that to her which made him even sexier, more endearing?

She swallowed hard. "Is that how you lure female executives away to prospective new companies—you charm them with sweet talk?"

"No, I sleep with them."

Paige's jaw dropped as she stared at him. Then she started to laugh when she saw the smile hovering on his lips and the teasing glint in his eyes. "Yeah, right." She glanced out the window and tried not to dwell on the fact that Matt currently wasn't involved in a relationship.

Since passing Portage La Prairie, the highway had wound through a region of rolling prairie and stands of spruce and basswood. It was beautiful and a sight to remember, but Paige was deeply aware that every kilometer they traveled brought her closer to the motel in Brandon and enhanced her guilt, inspiring definitely nonplatonic speculations, about what a night in Matt's arms would really be like.

TALKING WAS PAIGE'S ONLY recourse to keep her fantasies about sleeping with Matt from taking center stage in her thoughts. They talked about the kidnappings over dinner and spread the files all over the

motel room. And when Paige could bear the tension
no longer between them, she took the coward's way
out and told Matt she was tired and wanted to turn
in. Though her pregnancy ensured she fell asleep
quickly, she found herself wide awake before seven
and far too aware of Matt's bare hairy legs jutting
out from a twisted jumble of sheets in the bed across
from her.

He slept on his stomach, his face turned toward
her, his lean features made more boyish by the shadows created by the drawn drapes. Her heart twisted
and for a fraction of a second a fragment of a memory—of another man sleeping in another bed—materialized like a hazy apparition in her mind only to
skitter away into the darkness from which it had
come.

Nausea punched Paige sharply in the stomach and
she raced for the bathroom. But the vestiges of a
smile trembled on her lips when she splashed cold
water on her face a few minutes later. Another memory had surfaced…a man, who could surely only be
the baby's father. Her heart quivered alarmingly in
her chest. Paige gripped the edge of the counter and
concentrated on the emotions swirling in her. Yes,
fear was one of them. But whether the fear was gen-
erated by the man she'd fleetingly glimpsed or by the
prospect of facing whatever was so deeply sub-
merged in her subconscious, she couldn't say.

But she definitely felt encouraged that this road
trip with Matt would eventually give her the answers
she needed.

Matt was still sleeping when she exited the bathroom. Deciding she needed a piece of toast to settle
the queasiness still lingering in her stomach, Paige

quietly changed into a loose-fitting denim sundress and slipped her bare feet into comfortable sandals. Grabbing her purse and a jar of her chocolate hazelnut spread that she'd brought along, she let herself out of their motel room. The morning was glorious…the sun flexing its golden rays across the turquoise water of the pool in the motel's courtyard below. The coffee shop was located near the motel's front office. Paige decided to bypass the stairs leading down to the parking lot from the second floor and use the stairs nearest the office instead.

Her thoughts shifted to the unsettling image her memory had dredged up minutes ago. The man's face had been concealed in shadow, but the questions Matt had put forth to Susan Platham-Burke yesterday about her captors suggested Paige might gain some valuable clues if she focused on other details, other senses.

The bedroom for instance. Was it the man's home or a hotel room? Was it richly appointed or Spartan? Would something about the man's personal belongings or a glimpse of scenery out a window suggest where he lived? Paige lost herself in the questions pummeling her mind.

The rumble of wheels was the only warning she had before the maid's cart struck her and sent her tumbling over the rail of the second-floor balcony.

Chapter Seven

There wasn't time to scream. Paige just reacted, madly reaching for purchase on the white iron railing. Her fingers curled around the decorative spindles and she felt an excruciating tug as if her arm was being pulled from its socket. Her other hand latched onto another spindle in a death grip.

She was sickeningly aware of her legs thrashing around in midair as if trying to climb an invisible set of stairs. Below she heard two thuds as her purse and the jar of chocolate spread hit the concrete patio surrounding the pool.

"Help! Matt! Somebody help me, please!" she screamed as her fingers slipped an inch on the spindle. Matt would never hear her. He'd been sleeping when she left.

Paige looked down in desperation, hoping that if she fell, she'd land in the water of the pool, but no such luck. The pool was off by several feet. "Somebody help me, please!" she cried at the top of her lungs. "I'm going to fall!"

Doors snapped opened along the second and first floor.

"Here!" Paige called out. "I'm hanging off the

railing." Her fingers slipped treacherously on the wrought iron as they grew damp with sweat. "Matt! Help!"

The landing vibrated with footsteps. "Hold on, miss, help's coming," she heard a man say as the maid's cart was pushed out of the way.

"Hurry...I'm not sure I can hold on much longer."

Another voice sliced through the crowd. "Out of my way, now!"

Paige looked up as two tanned hands slipped between the rails and clamped around her wrists like manacles. "I've got you, sweetheart." Tears filled her eyes as she gazed into Matt's intense blue gaze. "I'm not letting go."

"Oh, Matt!"

"Trust me. You're going to be fine."

Paige didn't doubt him for an instant. With the assistance of several men and a sheet, she was pulled back up over the rail to a round of enthusiastic applause from the crowd. Matt's arms enveloped her in a protective embrace.

"You are one accident-prone handful," he murmured roughly against her ear. "Do you need an ambulance?"

She shook her head. The right side of her body throbbed dully where the cart had struck her and her shoulder sockets ached, but she didn't think anything was fractured. Only bruised. "I don't think so."

Paige thanked the men who'd helped in her rescue and warily scanned the crowd. There was no sign of a maid who must have been in charge of the cart. Only curious strangers gawking at her.

A trim elderly woman wearing a royal blue Hawaiian print robe climbed the stairs with Paige's purse. "I found this by the pool. The jar was broken so I threw it away."

Paige thanked her.

"My pleasure. I'm just glad you're okay. What happened, did you trip?"

"Not exactly—" Paige paused, not sure how to explain what had happened, particularly in front of a crowd of strangers.

Paige let her purse strap dangle from her fingers as she looked up at Matt. Her grandmother had told her once that handsome is as handsome does, and Matt Darby, scar and all, seemed far more handsome than any man had a right to be at this moment. Relief and gratitude and an emotion she didn't want to acknowledge welled in her heart. "This is getting to be a bad habit...your rescuing me."

"Don't I know it."

His thumb grazed her cheekbone in a tantalizing caress that unleashed ever widening rings of forbidden sensations as it spread through her body. Paige couldn't prevent herself from swaying into him until their thighs barely touched.

"What happened?" he demanded. "I thought we agreed I wasn't going to let you out of my sight..." That authoritative edge which had moved the crowd still clung to his tone, but underneath it, Paige heard proprietary concern. Or was he just not used to people disobeying his orders?

"The baby was hungry for chocolate hazelnut toast and I didn't want to disturb you," she said tartly, rubbing her sore hip. "How was I to know a housekeeper's runaway cart would ram me like a billy goat and turn me into a high-flying trapeze artist. The maid sure didn't hang around to rescue me or at least claim responsibility.''

Matt's brows knit together. ''That's assuming it was the maid who pushed the cart. Two freak accidents within a four-day period strike me as being a little too coincidental… Maybe we should talk to the maid and the manager of the motel. Maybe they saw someone or something suspicious.''

''And maybe they'll call the police who'll want to know why I believe someone wants to kill me.'' Paige gripped his arm, seized by a dawning sense of urgency. ''Let's just get out of here, please, Matt. We've obviously been followed.''

Suspicion wrapped around Hollis like velvet ribbons, suffocating him and leaving his soul aching with disappointment. Why was it every time he began to trust her, something happened which made him see himself for the world's biggest fool?

He clamped his fingers around hers. The only thing he knew was true was that she was pregnant and the baby she was carrying could be his. That alone was worth risking his neck and his sanity to find out why someone was trying to kill her. ''Okay, we'll go.''

WERE THEY BEING followed? Hollis glanced in the rearview mirror for what must be the millionth time in the last two days, checking the traffic behind them on the Trans-Canada Highway for a dark blue sedan resembling the car which had nearly run Paige over at the restaurant. He was getting damned paranoid and Paige was getting testy about his determined efforts to stick to her like glue, particularly when he hovered outside the ladies' rest-room door. But Hollis couldn't help it. Which made it all the more confusing how his father could have deserted him and his mother. Just walked away as if he didn't have a care in the world as to what would happen to them in the snake pit of the Hollis family.

A man didn't abandon his family no matter what. Even if he thought the woman he loved had betrayed him.

And he still loved Paige. The distrust rampaging in him like an ornery bull didn't change his feelings and didn't change the intense physical reaction he had to her body. Being with Paige was like savoring a glass of icy lemonade: the experience was tart, delicious and only temporarily quenched his thirst of her.

At least their efforts to retrace Paige's flight across the country hadn't resulted in the resurgence of any haunting memories of her being sexually assaulted by a stranger, which only made him more ruefully aware of how much, despite everything, he wanted Paige's baby to be his.

It was evening by the time they made it to Calgary, the Alberta city where Will Harper, the third kidnap victim lived. They checked into the same hotel Paige had stayed in previously. Somehow the sight of the perennially snow-dusted Canadian Rockies looming on the western horizon from their hotel room gave Hollis hope that this quest for Paige's memory would reach an end—one way or another—when they hit the Pacific Coast and Vancouver.

His disguise had fooled Paige, but he wasn't sure how well it would fool people he'd worked beside for years. Of course his family knew he was still alive, but Hollis wasn't sure he could trust them not to give him away.

"I'll try Will Harper's office again tomorrow morning," Paige said, determination glowing in her eyes as she looked up at him over the top of her menu in a steak house they'd found down the street from the hotel. A candle flickered in a ruby globe on the center of the thick plank table. "This time I'll get past his secretary. If that doesn't work, we can always wait for him outside his office building or his home. We could undertake a search of his media clipping ourselves, but I don't plan on leaving Calgary until we speak to him. His first-hand account will help Professor Zbarsky profile the kidnappers."

Hollis gave Paige's knee a warning nudge under the table as a man in scuffed up cowboy boots, skin-tight faded jeans and a T-shirt sporting a vulgar saying about women was seated in the booth directly across from them. The whipcord muscles of his physique gave him a hard as nails attitude. The man's eyes raised to challenge Hollis's interested gaze, but a filthy ball cap pulled low over the man's brow cast a shadow over the upper part of his face. Still, Hollis sensed a calculated cunning beneath that ball cap as the man's gaze swept over Paige, too. Then, with a faint polite nod in their direction, he lifted the menu.

Hollis glanced around the restaurant studded with lariats, wagon wheels and framed pictures of the Calgary Stampede. Ninety-five percent of the men in the restaurant were wearing cowboy boots. He really was paranoid.

"DAMN," PAIGE SIGHED, hanging up the phone the next morning. "I can't get past Harper's secretary. No media interviews. Unfortunately, the secretary neither confirmed nor denied whether I'd interviewed

Harper previously.'' She rose from the desk in their hotel room and turned to face Matt, who was stowing his shaving kit in his suitcase. She swallowed involuntarily at the sight of his clean-shaven jaw and the provocative scent of his sandalwood cologne. In preparation for their interview he'd paired a tailored gray windowpane checked sports coat with a bold red striped cotton dress shirt and black dress slacks. A red and black geometric silk tie her father would have highly applauded, made him look ready for a corporate takeover.

Or a very personal takeover of her heart. Paige firmly tamped down on the thought as being highly inappropriate.

''Prepare yourself,'' she went on. ''You're about to experience the paparazzi method of journalism….lying in wait and invading people's privacy in hopes of getting an interview. Not my preferred method.''

''Well, before you resort to that, why don't you let me try contacting Harper?'' Matt offered. ''I might be able to convince him to meet with a headhunter who has an interesting opportunity to present to him.''

''Oh, that approach certainly ranks higher on the ethical scale,'' Paige said dryly.

''What, you don't think he'll be interested in what I have to say?''

She motioned toward the phone. ''Be my guest.''

To her chagrin, Matt's tactic worked. Harper had room in his schedule, provided Matt could be there in half an hour.

''Why didn't you tell Harper the truth when you were put through to him?'' she demanded.

"Because he's so media spooked he would have changed his mind, no doubt."

"I suppose so. At least I know you can handle the interview by yourself. You were great with Susan Platham-Burke. I'll give you the file and my tape recorder."

"Thanks. The only thing I don't like about this plan is leaving you here alone. But Harper's secretary might recognize you if you come along. Promise me you'll stay in the room with the door locked and you won't unlock it for anyone."

"I promise," she grumbled.

"On your word of honor as a journalist?"

She glared at him. "Go already! I assure you I'll enjoy every second of my privacy."

Except Paige realized as soon as Matt left that she wasn't entirely alone. Her worries over the baby growing in her womb and the scent of Matt's cologne were her constant companions.

"I'LL GET RIGHT TO THE point, Harper," Hollis said, shaking hands with the lawyer who had worked himself up to the office of president in the Harper family's real estate investment company. "I'm on a mission to find the cutthroat bastards who think they can get away with taking us and our families hostage, not to mention help themselves to an undeserved chunk of our savings accounts."

Will Harper's grip tightened around Matt's fingers in a perceptible physical threat. The dark eyes in the handsome face narrowed shrewdly. "I'm afraid I don't understand, Mr. Darby. And you have approximately ten seconds to clarify your purpose for being here before I have security toss you out of here."

Hollis had no intention of engaging in hand-to-hand combat with Harper or the squadron of security he'd passed through to reach Harper's inner sanctum. "Matt Darby's an alias the police gave me after those bastards tried to blow me into kingdom come. My real name is Hollis Fenton."

Harper paled beneath his tan and released Matt's hand. "But you're supposed to be dead—"

"That's a little secret only you and a handful of other people are privy to. If you can't trust a lawyer to keep a matter confidential, who can you trust?"

"How do I know you're who you say you are?"

"Have your secretary put a call through to my Uncle Luther at the Hollis Group. Tell him he's listed as a personal reference for Matt Darby."

Harper placed the call himself, impressing Hollis with his facility with words as he wrangled the information he required out of Luther. He hung up the phone slowly and leaned back in his black leather chair. Folding one arm across his chest, Will Harper braced his elbow on the folded arm and curled his fingers into a fist which he tapped pensively against his lips. "So, Hollis Fenton, what do you want from me?"

"I want to compare notes about our ordeals. I've already spoken to Susan Platham-Burke, though I didn't identify myself because of the presence of a third party at the time. And I have information from a source close to the family about Claude Belanger's kidnapping. It's been six weeks since my abduction, which means the next kidnapping could take place in as little as three weeks. You strike me as being a smart man and I know I'm arrogant enough to think we have a chance of coming up with something that could give the police the lead they need to catch these creeps. The question is—are you game?'' Hollis glanced pointedly at the photo of a beaming, tooth-less baby wearing a pink frilly ballet costume on the lawyer's desk. ''You've got a lot to lose.''

Harper grinned soberly, pride lighting his face as he picked up the pewter-framed photograph. ''This is Emma. She's all the motivation I need.'' Hollis nodded, a knot of understanding forming in his gut as Harper buzzed his secretary and instructed her to hold his calls.

Hollis began with Professor Zbarsky's theory.

''Do the police know about this theory?'' the law-yer interjected, adjusting a pair of dark-rimmed read-ing glasses on his nose as he scanned the notations written on the newspaper clippings Hollis had given him.

''I haven't shared it with them as yet, but I'm sure they have their own experts who've drawn the same conclusions.''

''It gives added meaning to the last words they said to me, which were, 'Fortunately for you, you've set a good example for the others and you'll live to enjoy your retirement.''' Harper sifted through the pile of clippings. ''This certainly makes me want to avoid the media in any way, shape or form for the rest of my life. I haven't given an interview since my abduction. Why aren't there any pictures of you in the articles detailing your abduction and murder?'' he asked dubiously.

''Growing up in the Hollis family has given me a life-long aversion to having flashbulbs going off in my face. After my supposed death, Uncle Luther made certain no photos were to be released as a precautionary measure to minimize the risks of someone recognizing me. The police agreed for their own reasons.'' Hollis didn't explain what those reasons could have been. ''My uncle has considerable influence when he chooses to exercise it.''

''Obviously. I think you're right on the money about how we were individually selected. I'm convinced I was singled out because I'd been profiled in a local business magazine last October—about the time the kidnappers were probably shopping for a new target after the Platham-Burke kidnapping in August. That gave them a couple of months to learn my routine. Hell, I didn't think a thing of it when I drove into the garage and noticed the bulb was burnt out in the garage door opener. Only that I'd better change the bulb before Mary, my wife, came home. I didn't want her stumbling over stairs in her condition. They were on me the second I climbed out of the car. I got in a few good licks, but they eventually overpowered me. There were three of them. It was the blow to my head that finally did me in.''

''How do you think they learned your routine? Did you receive any suspicious phone calls or did anyone new enter your life or Mary's life a week or so before it happened?''

''I think they were watching the house. Mary went to a prenatal fitness class on Tuesday nights at five and she'd be home about six-thirty or quarter to seven. I'm usually home around six.''

Hollis let out the breath he'd been holding. No encounters with a gorgeous blonde with silver eyes and a dynamite smile.

''What can you tell me about your abductors?''

Hollis asked. "Did you notice any physical characteristics? Height, body build, hair color?"

"Well, before they put this hood on me I saw a gleam of gray hair—or at least it seemed that way in the dark. And one had gone to fat. My fist met with a fleshy stomach. The other two were leaner and definitely taller than my five feet eleven inches. It doesn't sound like much to go on, does it?"

"On the contrary. You've just confirmed details that Susan Platham-Burke observed. One definitely overweight. One possibly gray-haired. Anything else you noticed? What about their language skills? Education?"

"They weren't street thugs but they were doing the physical work themselves. I had the impression they were white-collar types with university degrees hanging on a wall somewhere. They didn't bully me or physically threaten me with their authority, which suggested they weren't from a military or law enforcement background. These men were coldhearted and deadly courteous. I had no doubt they had every intention of carrying out their threats if crossed. You're lucky you survived their reprisal."

"I'll feel luckier when they're in jail. Where'd they take you?"

"Outside the city. It was quiet. No traffic noises. Just the sounds of those bastards playing poker in another room, but they kept their voices low so I could never tell exactly what they were saying. Occasionally someone would drive off in the van and come back with food. I had a liquid diet. Straws only. They had me tied to a damn chair."

"Me, too." Hollis said. "Except one of them

found shoving food in my mouth an entertaining way to pass the time.''

"At least they let me relieve myself, though the gun pointed at the back of my head was a stress inducer. I never told Mary about that.''

"So you think you were in a house?''

"Definitely. Probably rented for that purpose. It was small. Two bedrooms, one bath. But it had a garage and a gravel driveway. The police have gone through a lot of effort in an attempt to locate that house. Unfortunately I was out for a while after they hit me, so I couldn't estimate how long it took us to get to the destination. All I could tell the police is that we were stuck in stop-and-go traffic for a while, but then Calgary is notorious for traffic jams.''

"Could you tell from the sound of their footsteps if they were wearing hard-soled or soft-soled shoes?''

"Soft-soled.''

"No cowboy boots?''

Harper arched a dark brow. "No. Why do you ask?''

"Because four men, not three, abducted me. And one of them definitely wore cowboy boots that left an impression on me in more than one spot.'' Hollis touched his ribs for emphasis. "Susan Platham-Burke was certain three men surrounded her.''

"So they brought in a fourth accomplice?''

"Yes. It's possible he was a participant all along and responsible for other duties, but they thought an extra pair of hands might be required because they had difficulty subduing you.'' Hollis paced the spacious office, thinking. "Were any footprints found at your release site that might indicate the number of your abductors?''

"No such luck. Two of them delivered me." Harper told Hollis the details of the million-dollar money exchange. After directing his brother through a wild-goose chase of phone calls made to his father's cell phone, the transaction had taken place during rush hour at a stop for the rapid transit C-train. "My brother was instructed not to turn around when someone tapped him twice on the back, just release the handle of the canvas bag he was carrying and keep walking or he'd be responsible for my death. They called the *Calgary Herald* three hours later and advised them of my release."

Hollis nodded. His uncle had told him that the kidnappers must have discovered the miniature tracking device the police had hidden in the seam of the canvas knapsack the kidnappers had insisted be used to carry the ransom money. "Claude Belanger's ransom drop was in a seedy warehouse district on the St. Lawrence River. But Susan's money exchange was similar to mine—a specific family member was told to walk out into an isolated wooded area. A voice called out to drop the money and leave. They never saw anyone. But there the similarities end. They demanded more money from my family—$1.5 million. The hood I wore was made out of a different fabric— mine was velvet, hers was cotton—and they didn't specify my release location when they called my secretary…which makes me think these bastards delight in keeping everything in flux."

"Hmm, either that or it's a copycat kidnapping," Harper mused. "You got any enemies?"

Hollis laughed dryly. He had a list of cousins who all wanted to be the crown prince. Not to mention his Aunt Evelyn who already saw herself as the queen of the Hollis Group. "Mostly family."

Harper didn't bat an eyelash. "Hey, I'm still in shock my brother didn't turn around. I suppose turning thirty matured him. For the record, my hood was made out of black cotton and had a hole cut in it by someone without tailoring skills. Have you spoken to Ellen Cummings in Halifax?"

"I haven't approached her yet," Hollis said. Ellen Cummings was the fourth kidnapping victim. Paige's trip had taken her west and Nova Scotia was twelve hundred kilometers east of Montreal. "Her kidnapping nixed the theory that the kidnappers were operating in an east-to-west pattern."

"Since her abduction was sandwiched between ours, she might be able to tell us if they upped her ransom demand or changed the fabric on the hoods. Perhaps she even noticed a fourth accomplice. I could try to get her on the speaker phone now if you like.... As they say, there's no time like the present."

Hollis nodded his consent, hoping Ellen Cummings might alleviate the embers of suspicion that smoldered in his core. Sure he distrusted his family, hated them sometimes, but beneath all that he still believed blood counted for something. His uncle and cousins had rallied behind him and paid the ransom, a gesture which had meant more to Hollis than he would ever dare admit to another living soul.

But the thought that one of them had had a hand in the terror of those fateful days left Hollis stonecold. If someone in his family was behind his kidnapping, they knew he was still alive. And they seemed determined to kill Paige before she remembered anything about the explosion.

"WHERE HAVE YOU BEEN?" Paige demanded, jerking open the door to their hotel room as he inserted the key card in the lock. The tiny welcoming flutter in her womb disconcerted her as she examined Matt from head to toe, relieved he appeared to be in one piece. And he had the audacity to grin at her after keeping her in unbearable suspense for four solid hours. She wasn't used to delegating tasks. Even to someone she trusted as much as Matt.

"Missed me, did you? How flattering."

Were her feelings that obvious? Paige groaned inwardly and decided evasion was the best way to deal with the veiled question hovering in Matt's eyes. "I'm starving! Thank heavens you brought food!" She snatched one of the two white paper sacks Matt juggled along with his briefcase, a sack that smelled of oil and vinegar and peppers and helped herself to a dill pickle nestled in a wax paper wrapper on the top of a couple of thick deli sandwiches. "Hmm. Delicious, but it needs chocolate," she said, crunching away.

"Wait a sec." Matt pulled a jar of her chocolate hazelnut spread from his jacket pocket.

Paige looked at the jar in his large tanned hand and inexplicably felt tears sting her eyes. "Thank you," she choked out, hating that she sounded like an emotional female. She could feel that their time together was coming to an end, and no matter how amicably they parted, it was going to hurt like hell. And the small stirring of memory she'd had in the motel suggested it could be very soon. It wasn't exactly like they were dumping each other. Just getting on with their lives. She took the jar from him and unscrewed the lid to satisfy the baby's odd craving.

"Quick, tell me what happened. Did you get it all on tape?"

Matt shook his head as he deposited his briefcase on one of the beds, then put the other sack on the table in the corner of the room and removed a soft drink and a carton of milk for Paige. "Harper's a lawyer—he declined."

"Figures." She joined him at the table as he unwrapped two enormous sandwiches. "Still, you must have had a lot to talk about. You were gone so long."

"I'm an inexperienced journalist, which is probably a good thing since he doesn't speak to the press. He didn't grant you an interview by the way. His security is more impressive than Miss Platham-Burke's. And it took longer because Harper made a conference call to Ellen Cummings in Halifax."

Paige dropped her pickle in the chocolate spread. "He what?" Alarm spiraled through her, nudging up her heart rate. The independent side of her nature wasn't sure whether she should be annoyed or tickled pink that Matt had succeeded where she had failed. Or maybe she was merely annoyed because he looked so dangerously hard-edged and sexy.

"He called Ellen Cummings and they compared notes of their kidnappings along with what I told them Susan Platham-Burke remembered and the information you gave me about Claude Belanger's kidnapping. I even have copies of the statements they gave to the police. And my briefcase is filled with newspaper clippings, including the one Will Harper is convinced singled him out as a prospective victim. Ellen Cummings faxed a pile to Harper's office, too."

"Oh, Matt, this is fabulous. We're really getting

somewhere. This might help us determine how the kidnappers find their victims. Maybe there's even a discernible pattern.'' She half rose from her chair intent on expressing her gratitude by brushing a kiss on his lean cheek. ''I could just…'' Her voice trailed off suddenly as the realization of what she intended brought a flash flood of embarrassment to her face.

''Just what?'' he demanded softly, leaning across the small table that separated them and lightly grasped her wrist. With a slight movement of his head his lips would fit securely on hers, as warm and compelling as the unmasked emotion simmering in his clear blue eyes, his kiss as wild as the dance of her pulse against his thumb.

Kiss you, Paige thought. *Throttle you for making me feel as if I need you. Blame you for making me wish the man I remember—the baby's father—is nobody special.* ''Just spend the rest of the day reading these,'' she answered brightly, remembering all the reasons why she couldn't allow another kiss between them to happen. Not now, maybe not ever. No matter how he looked at her or how broad his shoulders seemed or how divinely masculine he smelled. She'd used her time alone this morning productively and had recalled one detail from her memory flash of the man: a golden twining pattern in the comforter covering him. It wasn't much, but it was something. And she was painfully aware of the fourteen-day blank period in her schedule from the time she estimated she'd arrived in Vancouver to the day of the explosion where she didn't know where she'd been or with whom. She only had one receipt to account for her whereabouts—and that was a gas receipt. She gracefully retracted her hand from his grip.

Hollis smothered a smile at her subtle rejection. He couldn't fault her behavior. In fact, he admired her noble ideals toward her baby's father and her self-control. At least the telltale trembling of her hands as she lifted her sandwich to her lips reassured his ego she wasn't completely immune to him, even if she didn't know who the hell he was.

The conference call with Ellen Cummings hadn't been as enlightening as Hollis had hoped. She'd been so terrified she honestly couldn't say whether three or four men had abducted her. She'd only distinguished two distinct voices. But she thought she had an explanation for the change in fabric for the mask. Hers had torn when they forced it over her head. Her ransom, however, was one million dollars which led Hollis to wonder if the kidnappers had increased the ransom when they'd added the fourth man. Her statement didn't contain any further information.

As Hollis answered Paige's questions about his meeting with Will Harper, doubts assailed him. Assuming his kidnapping wasn't a copycat event, how had the kidnappers selected him? He'd always kept a low profile in the press…even more so after Christine's suicide. But of course, Pacific Gateway Shipping was occasionally noted in the business news and he might well have been mentioned in an article featuring one of his relatives. He'd ask Noreen to check it out when they got to Vancouver.

His eyes raked over Paige's glowing face and the mercurial shine in her eyes. His heart wrenched with a fierce need to protect her and the baby. Vancouver was the last place he wanted to take her. The place where it all began. And, he feared, the place where it could all end.

Chapter Eight

Paige felt an unfamiliar tension encase her in a clammy second skin as their route along the Trans-Canada Highway brought them closer to Vancouver. She felt soul-stirringly certain that the answers she was looking for lay at the base of those majestic snow-capped mountains in the distance.

She crossed and uncrossed her legs restlessly in the new rental car Matt had picked up in Calgary as a precautionary measure. She'd been surprised he drove a rental car, but he'd said since he traveled so much he preferred it to leasing or buying. Perspiration beaded on her face despite the sedan's air-conditioning. Her mouth felt dry with fear. Since they'd left on this cross-country journey nine days ago, she'd been waiting for something like this to happen—some inner warning system to tell her she was in danger. But the all-too-brief flashback she'd experienced in Brandon, Manitoba, hadn't prepared her for the sensation of panic that bore down insistently upon her chest. *Go home,* her mind seemed to scream at her.

"Matt, stop the car, please..."

Matt braked and swerved to the shoulder of the

two-lane highway. Before he'd brought the car to a complete halt, her hands were already on the latch, opening her door. The ripe scent of manure from the dairy farms in the Fraser Valley sent her reeling toward the ditch, where she promptly got sick.

"Here." A couple of facial tissues appeared over her right shoulder, courtesy of Matt.

"Thanks," she murmured.

"You okay?"

She shook her head, her eyes darting warily toward the mountains. "No. I can't go there, Matt. Whatever happened to me…whoever fathered my baby…it happened there…maybe in those blank two weeks before the explosion…maybe even when I left the hospital. I could have been attacked in the parking lot." Her chin quivered. "All I know is that there's this force inside me vehemently protesting the wisdom of me stepping foot in that city."

Hollis couldn't agree with her more. He gripped her arms and pulled her against him. Her limbs were stiffer than fence posts. "You feel it too, huh?"

"I'm so afraid, Matt."

He massaged her shoulders. "I know, sweetheart, but we've come this far. My mother told me once that courageous people have a healthy respect for fear and they do what's right regardless."

She made a moue of disagreement. "You called me sweetheart again."

"So I did."

"What if I find the baby's father…and I love him?" she asked, angling her chin up until her gaze locked with his. "I was there fourteen days before the explosion. That's plenty of time to fall in love. Maybe he didn't return my feelings which is why I haven't heard from him.'' She chewed on her lower lip. ''Or maybe he's been waiting for me to call, wondering why I dropped off the face of the earth.''

Hollis stilled, oblivious to the cars and trucks barreling past them and ached to tell her the truth and reveal his identity. But sadly, the only truth he knew was that it had only taken him a week to fall in love with her. He had no idea if she'd been involved with someone else at the time—perhaps one of the kidnappers. Only she had that knowledge locked inside her mind.

The intolerable prospect that she could be in love with another man gnawed at him. When he was a teenager in high school, he'd come home one night to find his mother had drunk herself into a rage. She'd told him that she'd loved his father enough not to beg him to return to her. That knowing he was happy made her misery bearable. Hollis had never understood his mother's logic until this moment.

He realized Paige was waiting for him to respond. ''If you find your baby's father and discover he will make you happy,'' he said slowly, ''then I'd say your courage paid off.''

''And what if I discover I was raped?''

''Then we'll both be grateful you survived and had the courage to face it.'' The wind whipped strands of gold silk around her cheeks. He traced his knuckles over the fragile line of her jaw, a grin tugging at his mouth. ''And I guess you'd no longer object to me calling you sweetheart.''

She blinked, then a tremulous smile darted over her kissable lips. ''You're all the courage I need, Matt Darby.'' With a defiant glare at the mountains she whirled around, dragging him toward the car by his arm. "Let's just hope that the fear of the unknown is more terrifying than the truth."

HOLLIS KNEW FULL WELL that Paige had stayed those forgotten two weeks at the Westin Bayshore Hotel—not that he'd allowed her to spend much time in her room. He took the liberty of checking them into the same hotel overlooking the shimmering deep blue waters of Coal Harbor and the Burrard Inlet, and the towering Douglas fir and red cedar groves of Stanley Park, hoping the scenery where they'd spent hours walking hand in hand might stir some memories for her.

Memories of the two of them and how incredibly good it had been. He didn't say a word after dinner when she told him she'd like to drive by the offices of Pacific Gateway Shipping on West Hastings Street and by the hospital where she'd been admitted after the explosion.

Hollis drove by the hospital first, where Paige stared out the car window for several minutes, then insisted they park in the parking garage. He walked with her through the structure, their footsteps echoing off the concrete walls, praying she hadn't been assaulted here—or anywhere else.

"You know, you could call that Vancouver police officer you mentioned. He could confirm whether they brought your car to the hospital," Hollis suggested, hoping Detective Boyle would inform Paige that Noreen had paid her hotel bill and brought her car to the hospital. Maybe just that bit of information would put a chink in the stone fortress protecting her memories.

"No, thanks. He already thinks I'm a nutcase."

His fingers loosely twined with hers and he noted with satisfaction that she didn't pull away from him. "Do you sense anything here?"

"No, my mind is frustratingly blank. Let's try the offices of Pacific Gateway Shipping."

Hollis went through the appropriate motions of finding his office building. He parked along the curb across the street from the sleek, gleaming skyscraper.

It was hard to believe the parking lot had resembled a war zone six weeks ago, carpeted with debris and shattered glass. The broken windows had been replaced with new sheets of gold-tinted glass, but scaffolding erected across the front of the building suggested ornamental repairs to the marine-theme frieze over the entrance were still underway.

Hollis's head throbbed as his memory brutally replayed that summer morning. The love that had buoyed in him at his first sight of Paige across the parking lot; the joy that crested, piquant and effervescent, as he'd run toward her—then the horror of a deafening roar obliterating it all.

He struggled to find his voice, to make words form that wouldn't reveal his fears. Despite all the doubts that still lingered, he couldn't stop himself from reaching out to her, needing her. He caressed her knee. "Do you recall anything?"

She shook her head, her jaw clamped shut.

"We could get out. Walk around." It was almost nine-thirty. The risk was small they might encounter someone he knew, who might recognize him despite the changes in his appearance.

"No." She closed her eyes and leaned her head against the headrest. "I think I just want to go back to the hotel, please."

Hollis stared at her. She was lying, he was sure of it. But why the hell wouldn't she tell him what was going on in her mind? Because she suspected something already? It took all his self-control not to let his anger show as he pressed on the gas and pulled away from the curb.

SHOCK AND HORROR were the only way Paige could describe the thick churning of emotions in her. When Matt had pulled up outside Pacific Gateway Shipping last night, the shadows stretching down between the office towers like dark slivers chipped from the dusky sky had seemed like grim fingers pointing out a stark and grisly truth.

She'd witnessed Hollis Fenton's death.

The knowledge sank into her, writhing with insinuations. Maybe her head injury was the sole cause of her amnesia, but Paige feared that she'd subconsciously erased the details of the shipping president's death because it had traumatized her so deeply she didn't want to remember. She, who'd always thought of herself as a tough, independent, thoroughly modern woman, was a coward. Whatever she'd seen that tragic morning might help the police catch the people who'd murdered Claude and Hollis Fenton.

But that might never happen unless all her memories returned. Not to mention that she might never know who fathered her baby if she couldn't summon up the inner strength to face those horrible memories again. She didn't understand all the complexities of how the mind worked, but if her mind had chosen to selectively block out that six-week period of her life, she presumed she wouldn't be able to recall anything until she faced whatever painful memories had erected the barrier.

Thinking of Brenda Thompson's need for justice for her husband's murder gave Paige the courage to call the offices of Pacific Gateway Shipping the next morning. Matt gave her an encouraging smile from the balcony, where he stood watching the activity in the marina below. Her resolve bolstered, she asked for the name of Hollis Fenton's personal secretary. The receptionist told her she'd connect her to Noreen Muir.

"Pacific Gateway Shipping. Evelyn Hollis-Styles's office. May I help you?" a voice crisp as a tart apple responded.

Paige's heartbeat went haywire with anxiety as she introduced herself.

"Ms. Roberts, how nice of you to call." The crispness softened to genuine concern. "How are you?"

Confusion swirled in Paige's thoughts. This woman spoke to her as if she knew her. "It's a long story," Paige said awkwardly. "In fact, I'm in Vancouver on personal business and I was hoping I might speak privately with you about Mr. Fenton's death."

"I see. In that case, I think it would be too unsettling for you to come here. Why don't I meet you for lunch? Where are you staying?"

Paige told her.

Noreen made a small harumphing sound Paige couldn't interpret and suggested they meet at a restaurant not far from Pacific Rim Shipping. "I'll make reservations for twelve-thirty. Will that suit you?"

"Yes, except that you'll want to make that reservation for three." Paige paused. "A friend of mine will be joining us."

"Of course."

Paige hung up the phone and splayed her fingers over her belly, perplexed by the meaning of Noreen Muir's warm reception. Goose pimples peppered Paige's arms. She had an intuitive feeling it would be a very enlightening lunch.

THE RESTAURANT WAS in a turn-of-the-century bank building, the marble decor opulent to the degree that Paige felt inclined to speak in hushed tones.

She unconsciously hung back behind Matt's lean frame as a dignified woman in a tailored navy suit, her stern features and sharp-toothed smile softened by a cap of soft white curls, entered the foyer and approached them, her hand outstretched. "Ms. Roberts. You're looking much improved over the last time I saw you. You gave me such a fright when you left the hospital without a word."

"Noreen?" Paige accepted the secretary's bony hand like a lifeline. In two sentences Noreen had already revealed so much. Paige had to take a steadying breath to keep herself from blurting out a slew of questions until the social niceties were dispensed with. "This is my friend and research associate, Matt Darby."

Noreen gave Matt a comprehensive sizing up and a brisk nod. "How do you do, Mr. Darby? I'm glad you brought him along, dear. You're trembling. I'll insist they seat us straight away."

Paige exchanged a questioning look with Matt as Noreen issued orders to the restaurant staff. They were immediately shown to a private table. Paige felt better with the firm support of the luxuriously cushioned chair beneath her and a glass of ice water within reach to soothe the nervous dryness in her mouth. Matt's hand placed surreptitiously on her thigh beneath the linen-draped table, helped, too. Its steady and unwavering warmth reminded her that no matter what Noreen told them, she had someone she could turn to if she needed him.

Paige primly moved his hand away, if only to prove to herself she was strong enough to face this on her own. Noreen's stern features couldn't disguise her compassion as Paige explained the extent of her amnesia and her attempts to fill in the gaps in her memory.

"I think I can answer some of your questions, Ms. Roberts. To the best of my recollection, you had an interview with Mr. Fenton on June twenty-fifth. I could check Mr. Fenton's appointment book to tell you the exact time if you like."

"That won't be necessary." Paige's pulse raced. June twenty-fifth was a week before Fenton's abduction.

"However, you apparently made quite an impression on him because he agreed to meet you the morning of the explosion. You didn't have a scheduled appointment, but Mr. Fenton informed me he was only coming into the office for a short time and planned to take the rest of the day off because he would be meeting you."

"I see." Paige wasn't sure what to make of this information. "I don't suppose I left a phone number where Mr. Fenton could reach me?"

"Certainly. You left the number of your hotel— the Westin Bayshore. You obviously don't recall this, but after the explosion I saw to it that your hotel bill was paid and your luggage packed and delivered to the hospital along with your car.''

''You paid my hotel bill?'' Paige squeaked, for the moment bypassing the shock that she and Matt had coincidentally chosen the same hotel.

Noreen looked uncomfortable and glanced down as the waiter delivered salads to the table. ''Not me personally, Pacific Gateway Shipping. Luther Hollis felt it the least we could do under the circumstances…with you being injured in the explosion that killed Mr. Fenton.''

Which explained why the secretary was being so accommodating. Was the shipping company and The Hollis Group hoping to avoid a lawsuit? Paige treaded delicately. ''I appreciate the thoughtfulness, though I wonder if you could tell me if my laptop computer and my briefcase were in my hotel room. They seem to have disappeared.''

Noreen looked stricken. ''I'm terribly sorry. I packed your things myself—perhaps somehow I overlooked them… We'll reimburse you for them if they've disappeared.''

Worried Noreen would be held accountable for the loss, Paige hastened to assure her that wouldn't be necessary. ''I'm still hoping they'll turn up somewhere. I'm determined to get my memory back. I want to do whatever I can to help the police discover who's behind these kidnappings. I thought perhaps if I saw a picture of Mr. Fenton it might trigger something… There were no pictures of him in the newspaper articles I've collected.''

''Mr. Fenton was never one to bask in the limelight. He told me he had enough difficulty dealing with the arrogance he'd inherited from his mother's side of the family, his ego couldn't tolerate the extra attention from the media." She smiled fondly, her eyes darkening with moisture as her gaze flickered from Paige to Matt. "I'll see what I can do about getting you a photo. I'll need permission from—" Noreen broke off abruptly.

"Pardon me for interrupting, but I thought that was you, Noreen."

Paige caught a whiff of musky cologne and glanced over her shoulder to see a balding, barrel-chested man in a dark superbly tailored suit, leaning heavily on a cane carved with a fearsomely distinctive wolf's head...the work of a talented West Coast Salish artist, no doubt.

"Ken Whitfield, you old darling. How are you?" Noreen rose and kissed the man's flaccid cheek. "I saw you at the funeral but there was no time to talk properly... It would have meant a lot to Hollis to know you'd come."

"I just wish I'd made an effort to make amends sooner. First Christine, now Hollis. It's terribly difficult to be so old and see these young people departing this earth before us. I don't even have any grandchildren to live for."

Maybe it was the dressing in the salad or the scent of Whitfield's cologne or the growing awareness that Noreen was obviously talking to Hollis Fenton's father-in-law, but Paige felt her stomach lurch. Matt had his head bent over his salad. Paige suspected he was trying, like her, not to eavesdrop on Whitfield's generous offer to make a sizable contribution to the Hollis Fenton Memorial Fund. Paige nudged Matt's arm with her elbow. "I'm going to the ladies' room for a few minutes. Can you ask the waiter to remove my salad? It's not agreeing with me.''

"Sure," Matt whispered in her ear. "Though, I'll come with you to—"

"Matt, really, it's not necessary."

"Shh, you're drawing attention and their conversation is affecting my appetite, too."

Thank heavens she bought his excuse, Hollis thought, trying to edge away from the table with Paige, before his father-in-law got more than a cursory glance at him. This was not the time to test whether Christine's father could see beneath the blue contact lenses, the broken nose and the military haircut.

He hadn't spoken to Ken since Christine's funeral. There had been too much anger and blame-hurling between them—and hurting each other wouldn't bring back Christine. Hollis felt humbled by Ken's gesture and hoped it was a sign of peace and forgiveness. When he returned to the land of the living, he'd have to offer his own olive branch to Ken.

Paige disappeared into the ladies' room looking decidedly green around the gills. Hollis loitered in the hallway near the pay phone and worried about her. But he figured he'd draw far too much attention to himself if he barged into the ladies' room. How long did nausea last during pregnancy? Three months? Longer?

He was deeply relieved when he saw Noreen briskly coming toward him.

She heaved a breathless sigh. ''That was close,'' she whispered. 'I don't think Ken recognized you. I, frankly, have difficulty believing my golden boy lurks somewhere beneath those blue eyes and that despicable haircut. That battered nose will take some getting used to. I told Ken you and Paige were my brother's son and wife, visiting from Scarborough. Is everything all right? Where's Paige?''

Hollis hesitated about telling Noreen about Paige's pregnancy. He trusted her more than anyone else on this earth. In many ways she'd been a substitute mother to him, but she also had a mind of her own and was infernally doing things she thought were for his own good—despite his orders. ''Paige isn't feeling well. Would you mind going in the ladies' room and checking on her?''

''Of course. But before I do, there's something I wanted to pass on. Something you must know.'' She looked back over her shoulder as though making certain no one was approaching and they were still alone. ''The police have traced the cell phone used as the power source in the bomb. You're not going to believe this, but they've traced the cell phone to your cousin Sandford. He reported it stolen in mid-May.''

Sandford? Aunt Evelyn's son. Hollis clenched his fists. Damn, what the hell did this mean? Was he dealing with a copycat crime or were the kidnappers already circling that close in May, making plans in case the ransom wasn't paid or Uncle Luther lived up to his reputation and tried to pull a fast one?

''The police took Sandford in for questioning, but they released him. What do you want me to do about the photo Paige requested?''

''Give it to her.''

''But—''

''It's a risk,'' he said curtly, growing tired of all the lies. ''But she needs to arrive at the truth on her own without us telling her. Maybe the photo will jar something. Now, please, go in and check on her.''

Noreen paused, her palm pressed to the door. ''Hollis?''

''Yes?''

''It's good to see you in love again. The moment I saw her I knew she was the right kind of girl for you.''

''I thought so, too.'' Hollis smiled grimly. ''Let's just hope she still feels that way after she finds out I'm a lying son-of-a-bitch. Now, get in there before I fire you.''

''I'm afraid you can't fire me. You're dead, remember?''

Hollis opened his mouth to protest, then snapped it closed in frustration. Noreen, as usual, was unerringly correct. He *was* dead and he wouldn't feel alive again until he knew for certain Paige loved him.

''HERE, DEAR, TRY THIS handkerchief. It might be better for removing the stain from your dress than that paper towel.''

Paige took the scrap of Irish lace Noreen offered. ''Thank you. I don't know what came over me. I think I'm coming down with the flu.''

''Flu, piddle. Your color isn't high like you have a fever. You're white as a sheet. I'd wager you're expecting.''

Paige mouth trembled. She pumped a dab of pink soap onto the handkerchief. ''Is it that obvious?''

''I've been around enough pregnant women to know the symptoms. Is that nice Mr. Darby the father?''

''Matt? No, we're not, I mean, we're friends but

not involved that way…'' Her voice trailed off. She scrubbed furiously at the spot. She might not have had color in her cheeks a moment ago, but they were vibrantly flushed now.

''Pity, he's very handsome in a rugged sort of way. He seems quite taken with you.''

''He's been wonderful. The truth is, Noreen, I've no idea who fathered my baby. I thought I might have been raped after I'd been released from hospital. Now, I'm not so sure. I think whoever he was, I met him here in Vancouver.'' She stopped scrubbing the spot to peer at Noreen. ''I don't suppose I'd been sharing my hotel room with anyone?''

''No-o.''

The secretary's slight hesitation made Paige suspicious. ''I didn't want to ask this in front of Matt, but did I have a personal relationship with your boss?''

''I wouldn't know. You had lunch together that first day. If something intimate developed from that meeting, the matter was entirely between you and Mr. Fenton. However, I can assure you Mr. Fenton wasn't the kind of person who acted irresponsibly.''

''Neither am I,'' Paige said stiffly, wondering if the woman was backpedaling out of fear she'd launch a paternity lawsuit.

''Of course you aren't. Anyone with eyes can see you're a sensible young woman.''

''But you will give me a photo of him?''

''Yes. I'll send one round to your hotel, though it might take some time to dig one up. He didn't like having his photo taken. But, I'm happy to do whatever I can to ensure Mr. Fenton's killers spend the rest of their miserable lives behind bars.''

"Good, because Mr. Darby and I have a few favors to ask and you're the only one who can help us. I've had three very close calls in the last eleven days and if it weren't for Matt, we wouldn't be having this conversation. Someone is trying to shut me up and I'm going to find out why before they succeed."

Noreen gasped. "What type of close calls?"

Paige told her in brief detail as she scrubbed at her dress.

"Promise me you'll be very careful in the future," Noreen admonished.

"I will. Matt thinks we lost them on the road after we changed cars in Calgary." Paige made one last dab at the damp spot on her dress with the handkerchief and decided she looked decent enough to return to the table.

Matt, bless him, had ordered her a fruit plate and a whole wheat roll.

True to her word, Noreen was receptive to cooperating with their investigation and related the details of the statement Hollis Fenton had made to the police regarding his kidnapping. Paige frowned when Noreen insisted four men had abducted Hollis Fenton from the seawall, jammed a black velvet hood over his head and transported him in the trunk of a car. She wondered what conclusions Professor Zbarsky would draw from the addition of a fourth man and the subtle changes in the kidnappers' modus operandi...the switch from a cotton to a velvet hood, the use of a sedan rather than a van and the kidnapping taking place on a Saturday morning rather than a Monday or Tuesday. Did the changes matter if the results remained the same and the kidnapping fit the signature of Professor Zbarsky's theory?

Just one little fact bothered Paige. How on earth had the kidnappers singled out Hollis Fenton if he habitually avoided the press?

As usual, Matt seemed to be on the same wavelength. He propped an elbow casually on the table. "If Professor Zbarsky's theory holds weight, Noreen, the kidnappers must have selected Hollis Fenton from a recent article written up about his shipping company—or possibly saw his name mentioned in an article profiling another member of the Hollis family. Does anything come to mind?"

"I'm sure there have been one or two items in *The Globe and Mail*," Noreen replied thoughtfully.

"Of course. It makes perfect sense that the kidnappers could be reading Canada's business paper cover to cover," Matt muttered. "I don't know why I didn't think of it earlier. Most of the major companies post appointment notices as a matter of course."

Noreen cleared her throat like a general about to plan a major assault on enemy lines. "I'll call *The Globe and Mail* and have an archival search done to make sure I haven't missed anything about Mr. Fenton. In fact, I could request name searches on all the victims if you think that would help. I've occasionally requested those type of searches when Pacific Gateway Shipping enters into dealings with companies we're not familiar with, particularly when there's a new CEO. The information is usually faxed to you within two days."

"That's a logical place to start," Paige agreed, "and it effectively spreads a net across the country. But just to make sure we cover all the bases in the local business news and the society pages, I think Matt and I should go down to the archives of *The*

Vancouver Sun after we're finished here and order a similar search done on the names of the victims. *The Vancouver Sun* is part of Canada's largest newspaper group and their archives can readily access any articles about a person in the same chain, anywhere in the country. It'll be more thorough than the searches I've done on the Internet.'' She crossed her fingers, determination flaring in her, brilliant and shimmering as a star in an inky sky. ''The kidnappers are smart, organized and meticulous. If we're very lucky, somewhere in those articles we'll find a pattern as to how they think.''

PAIGE POPPED HER HEAD off the pillow the second Matt slipped into the bathroom and closed the door. She'd been waiting ages for him to wake up and start his morning routine. For a man with such a Spartan haircut and a lean physique, he spent a great deal of time in the shower. And she was counting on him being in there for a good twenty minutes, which should be plenty of time to make a covert trip to the lobby. During a middle-of-the-night trek to the bathroom, she'd found a note on the carpet in front of the door that informed her she had a courier delivery waiting for her at the front desk. Noreen must have found a photo of Hollis Fenton.

Paige wanted her first glimpse of Hollis Fenton to be private. If she'd had a relationship with him she didn't want to discover it under Matt's watchful eyes. She hadn't slept the rest of the night…thinking about that photo and what it might mean. She hastily pulled on her denim sundress and sandals, then finger-combed her hair. The shower went on in the bathroom as she grabbed her purse. She tried to divert her mind from an image of Matt standing naked beneath a pulsing spray of hot water and decided her clandestine mission was well-timed. Still, a nervous tremor rocked through her as she threw the lock and eased the door open. She had another bit of private business she wanted to accomplish at the front desk without Matt as an interested audience.

Her heart leapt to her throat when the front desk clerk handed her the cardboard envelope. What if she didn't recognize Hollis Fenton? What if she did? Paige set the envelope aside on the counter and asked for a copy of her hotel bill from her previous visit spanning the last week of June and well into July. The clerk was happy to oblige her. Paige felt as if she'd hit pay dirt when she saw the detailed list of local and long-distance calls she'd made. The paper trail of these phone calls would tell her something…even if the photo did not.

The photo…

Thanking the clerk, Paige clutched the envelope and the hotel bill to her chest and walked outside, seeking a secluded spot to view the photo. The morning was cool. Low gray clouds hovered over the Burrard Inlet and masked the view of the North Shore mountains. Paige shivered involuntarily as she headed toward a row of benches near the marina.

She told herself as she sat down that knowing the truth would be better than living in the haze of uncertainty that had defined her life these last six weeks. Stomach clenched, she removed the eight-by-ten photo from the envelope.

It was an executive portrait. Regret and a searing sense of loss lanced her soul at her first glimpse of the man who was as heart-stoppingly photogenic as the other victims. Hollis Fenton was unsmiling, his hazel eyes steady with determination beneath a shock of shining blond hair. Something about his hair aroused a surge of undeniable recognition that made her head pound…

Suddenly she could see the man in the bed again, a duvet with an intricate rope design bunched at his waist as he slept. His features were still shadowed, but she could make out the shimmering fringe of his hair in the moonlight and sense its silken texture in her fingers. Then the memory vanished, leaving her deeply bereft.

Paige wept as she traced the line of Hollis Fenton's straight, noble nose and his gold-tipped brows with her finger, knowing instinctively that this was something she'd done once in the flesh. She didn't have to check out the telephone numbers on the hotel bill to know she literally held her heart in her hands. She hadn't been raped. Hollis Fenton had given her this keepsake baby.

And she'd cared enough about him that her mind had dealt with the traumatic shock of his death by blocking out the details of the trip that had led her into his arms.

Wiping at her tears, Paige jokingly told herself that she must have a thing for men with square jaws, because Matt had a square jaw as well, though he didn't possess Hollis's patrician features. Still, Matt had the same kind of commanding presence that radiated from Hollis's photo. The kind of presence that stirred an immediate response from her—both emotionally and physically. She gazed down into Hollis Fenton's gold-flecked hazel eyes and silently promised him she'd remember everything. For herself. And for their baby. Then she put the photo and the receipt in the envelope and started back to the hotel.

She didn't hear the car jump the curb and bear down the wide sidewalk toward her until it was almost upon her.

Chapter Nine

Where was she?

Feeling thoroughly disgruntled, Hollis yanked open the door of their room and scanned the corridor in both directions. Paige had obviously dressed quickly. Had she gone to get some ice? Or had an overpowering craving for food? He raked his fingers through his damp hair. Hell, she'd promised she'd stay within his sight. Given him her *word*. Maybe she'd called to him while he was in the shower and he hadn't heard her.

Hollis wheeled around back into the room to finish dressing. He saw the scrap of paper peeking out beneath Paige's pillow when he snagged his watch off the night table between their beds.

A delivery…? Then, he remembered the photo Noreen was supposed to send and the pieces fit together. Paige had obviously gone down to the front desk to get the photo and the fact she'd hidden the note under her pillow clearly indicated she didn't want him to know.

Which meant she must have some suspicions.

Hollis sank down onto the edge of the bed to wait. Had the time of reckoning finally come?

THE WILL TO SURVIVE and to save Hollis's baby sent Paige jumping feet first into the bitter cold saltwater of the marina. Her denim dress billowed up around her head on her plunge into the water, then grew heavy as she struggled upward to swim to the surface.

But surfacing made her feel vulnerable.

Shivering and gasping for breath, Paige tread water and warily eyed the rock-screed embankment that dropped abruptly down to the water's edge from the sidewalk. There was no sound of a commotion on West Georgia Street above her. But it was early on a Saturday morning and traffic was scarce. Maybe no one had witnessed the car forcing her into the water. And whoever had tried to kill her had probably kept on driving. Paige had no doubt someone was trying to kill her. The question was—why? Was someone hunting her down because of something she'd witnessed the morning of the bombing or because she carried Hollis's child?

Hollis. The courier envelope bobbed in the water along with her purse; Hollis's photo undoubtedly ruined. Paige collected them and swam toward the embankment. The sooner she spoke to Professor Zbarsky about the inconsistencies she'd noted yesterday when Noreen had recounted Hollis Fenton's kidnapping, the better she'd feel.

Now she just wanted to get safely back to her room, a hot shower and Matt.

HOLLIS LEANED AGAINST the door, his jaw slack as he took in Paige's drenched appearance. Her hair clung to her head in ropes and a damp spot formed on the carpet beneath her feet. Tightly clenched in her fingers was a sodden cardboard envelope. He didn't know what he'd expected upon her return—fury, outrage, disillusionment, but certainly not that she'd feel so betrayed she might want to punish him by jumping off the Lion's Gate Bridge.

Was this Paige's version of don't get mad, get even?

Hollis clamped his jaw shut as bile rose in his throat. He'd never have thought Paige would hit so far below the belt as to remind him how Christine had ended her life.

"Don't say anything," she warned, marching past him.

Uh-oh. That didn't sound good, but Hollis didn't trust himself to speak anyway. Mutely, he followed her into the room where she dumped her purse and the envelope on a dresser. Her purse, he noticed, was soaked, too.

His stomach tensed into a taut wall of anxiety.

Paige's fingers fumbled uselessly with the buttons on her dress, but damn the woman, she remained silent. Were her teeth chattering from anger or cold?

"You're freezing, your lips are blue," he said curtly when he couldn't stand the mounting silence drumming against the walls a second longer. "Get those wet clothes off. I'll turn the shower on for you."

"No, wait! I—I should never have left the room without you. A car tried to mow me down—"

Hollis ignored the rest. He didn't know who moved first, but suddenly Paige was in his arms and he was fitting her snugly to him as if only having her this close could keep the fear that gnawed his heart at bay. Her wet dress soaked his T-shirt and trousers, but he didn't give a damn. Her soft curves fit into all the right places.

He threaded his fingers through her hair to keep his hands from seeking the swells of her breasts and the turgid buds of her nipples pressing intimately into his chest. Lord, he didn't want to think that she was probably naked underneath her dress. "Thank God, you're okay. Did you get a license plate or anything?"

She shook her head. "But the car was a black Volvo and there was one man in it." The tremor that wracked her frozen body vibrated into him, stirring concern and an overwhelming desire to warm her with his flesh. "I jumped into the marina to get away."

Did that mean she hadn't looked at the photo at all? That he still had time to hold her? Kiss her? Maybe there was another way to stimulate her memory. He pressed a kiss on her chilled brow. Her skin tasted faintly of salt, but to him it was a sweet forbidden nectar. "I like a woman who can think on her feet," he murmured huskily, half expecting her to stop him or pull away as he laid a heated trail of kisses along her temple and down the delicious curve of her cheek.

Paige arched into him and Hollis felt his senses explode at the full tantalizing imprint of her body against him. Despite the dampness of their clothes, a compelling heat radiated between their bodies like stones casting off the golden heat of the sun's rays. His fingers clamored to caress, to feel, to stroke every silken and mysterious inch of this tempting woman who so dominated his thoughts and frustrated him to the depths of his soul. Hollis had learned in his marriage to Christine that love was all about difficult decisions and Hollis hovered on the brink of yet another decision. Paige might not remember him, but would her heart remember his touch and the shattering passion of their lovemaking? She'd dug her nails into his shoulders and cried out his name when he'd parted her trembling thighs and tasted the sweetness of her...

Hollis pulled back, aching with restraint. "You're safe now. Let's get you into the shower before you catch pneumonia."

"Yes, you irritating man. I'm finally ready to concede that I shouldn't have gone out without you." Her chin jutted up and pure mischief, rather than anger, glowed in her eyes as her palm slid provocatively over his chest and cupped the back of his neck. "But I'm mature enough to admit when I'm wrong and learn from my mistakes. I'm not going into the shower unless you come with me."

With a jolt of surprise, Hollis felt the pressure of her soft, full lips purposively sweep his jaw and seek his mouth as the meaning of her words sunk into his addled brain.

He met her kiss tentatively, thrown off by this sudden reversal in her behavior. Did she..? But when her tongue darted seductively into his mouth in a bold invitation, Hollis stopped thinking and reacted with his body. With a feral growl, he deepened the kiss, unleashing the need and the doubts that had been festering in him since he'd regained consciousness in the hospital.

Paige locked her arms around Matt's neck, prepared to hang on for dear life. Matt's kiss was an explosion of sensuous strokes: it irritated, it soothed, it excited, it cajoled, it demanded more emotionally from her than any kiss had ever demanded of her. She gave back one hundred percent and still it wasn't enough. He wanted more from her than this and she was ready to give it. Somehow she felt Hollis had sent her a guardian angel in the form of Matt to look after her and the baby. She wasn't going to question it.

She strained against Matt's hand as it curved proprietarily over her breast, whimpering as his gentle kneading made her sensitive flesh feel achy and full. When the pad of his thumb brushed her swollen nipple through the wet denim she nearly swooned. Oh, what was he doing to her?

His warm breath brushed her ear and sent a tingle of goose bumps rising along her spine. ''There's more to come, sweetheart. Let's get you out of these wet clothes.''

''You, too,'' she insisted, frantically pulling his T-shirt out of the waist of his trousers as he worked the buttons of her dress. His arousal bulged against the zipper of his trousers. Paige boldly touched him and felt him surge into her palm through the thick material. His response felt as primitive and unrestrained as the wild desire teeming through her.

''Careful, sweetheart, you're torturing me,'' Matt whispered huskily, peeling her dress down off her shoulders.

''I think that's the whole idea,'' she quipped, pushing the dress over her hips until it fell in a damp heap at her feet. Paige kicked off her sandals and stood in front of him totally bare, shivering in anticipation of the hunger in his gaze.

Matt sucked in his breath. ''You're so gorgeous.''

His knuckles traced the curve of her belly in a gesture so gentle and deferential to the baby Paige felt her bones melt. How she'd resisted him this long she had no idea. "I knew you weren't wearing anything beneath that dress."

"I guess I can't hide anything from you—"

"Definitely not." His fingers splayed over her hips as if determined to prove he was more than capable of conducting a thorough hand search.

Paige wasn't going to let him have all the fun. "You, however, still have a big secret." She eased his zipper down, smiling when Matt shuddered as she shimmied his trousers and briefs over his rock-plated thighs. The man had legs to die for—and a few other perfectly sculpted body parts, too...

She gasped as he scooped her up, thwarting her own exploration and carried her into the bathroom. Feminists didn't let men sweep them off their feet, did they? Maybe they should, she decided as Matt stepped into the shower with her and turned on the tap.

Warm water pummeled their bodies. "This will heat you up on the outside." Matt grinned and reached for the bar of soap. "I'm in charge of the rest."

A knot of blissful emotion formed in her throat. When he suggested she turn around, his wicked grin made her heart trip in nervous anticipation as she presented her back to him. Just what did he have in mind?

Matt's hands were slick and sure as he soaped her shoulder blades in circular, sensuous strokes, then played down her spine to massage her buttocks. Paige reached behind her, bracing her palms on his thighs as a flurry of sensations began to coalesce in her midriff. His hands smoothed over her shoulders and ran down over her ribs to feather the undersides of her breasts until the soft swells ached with need at his teasing. Paige moaned, pressing her buttocks into Matt's hardness when his fingers caught a dusky, pebbled tip and teased it, rolling it between his thumb and forefinger.

"Ah, so I have your attention," he murmured, nibbling her shoulder.

Paige curled her fingers around his smooth shaft. "Just as I have yours."

"That's what I like about you—you're an equal opportunity player." Matt's fingers brushed her inner thighs. "Open for me, sweetheart. Let me touch you."

Paige parted her legs. Tension, taut and sweet, hummed in her as he stroked the pale curls of her femininity and slid a finger into her moistness. Nothing had ever seemed more erotic to her than this touching and the words Matt whispered in her ear as he brought her higher and higher.

She writhed against him. "Kiss me, please."

"Soon, sweetheart, I want to hear how I'm pleasing you. Tell me what you like." With infinite skill, he found the ultrasensitive nub at the central core of her tension and Paige told him exactly what she liked until her thoughts scattered and her world fragmented and she was shuddering in Matt's arms.

Knees weak, she turned and greedily sought his kiss beneath the warm mist of the shower. He smelled of soap and clean male. This kiss, like the last, was as potent as the words he'd murmured in her ear. The taste of him so familiar...as if he'd always been a part of her. She ran her fingers over his muscled shoulders and the newly healing scar on the sharp ridge of his chest, pulling him closer. He was no longer wearing the bandage. His skin felt sleek and hard like polished oak. And so fiery hot.

Paige couldn't remember ever wanting a man like this, to the point where all she could think about was having him inside her. Had she wanted Hollis this much? She touched her lips to Matt's ruggedly bumpy nose. He might not have Hollis's golden boy good looks, but he made up for it in a hefty dose of unadulterated sex appeal.

Matt lifted her high against him and Paige instinctively wrapped her legs around him, hooking her heels on his calves. Water danced over his broad shoulders and splashed onto her face. With a deep sigh of satisfaction, she lowered herself onto him, the fit so perfect and hot and tight. Clenching muscles she didn't realize she possessed, she shifted her hips and a five-alarm sensation of mind-reeling pleasure raked her from her fingers to her toes.

"Oh, sweetheart, the things you do to me," Matt groaned against her mouth, clasping her bottom and thrusting deeply into her.

Paige gripped his tanned shoulders and rode the wave of his male heat. Then she deliberately clenched those muscles and rotated her hips, creating a friction so heavenly it took her breath away. "Just wait," she panted, matching his next thrust, "the best is yet to come."

The water drowned out Matt's hoarse cry as she demonstrated just what she had in mind.

PHYSICALLY AND EMOTIONALLY spent, Hollis pulled the sheet up and tucked it around Paige's freckle-kissed shoulders as she burrowed into his side. Guilt tarnished the halcyon contentment of being physically close to her again. Only time would tell if he'd made a serious tactical mistake by making love to her. Not that he'd been capable of offering any resistance at the time...

"I should have known once wouldn't be enough with you," he reflected, wrapping a damp tendril of her freshly washed hair around his finger, ignoring his growling stomach. They'd skipped breakfast and it was almost noon, but he didn't want anything to intrude on the intimacy of the moment.

Her head darted up. "Are you complaining?"

"Never." Hollis laughed and kissed the tip of her nose. "Just awed." And he was awed. The new fullness in her breasts had intrigued him as had the idea that her belly and her slim hips would swell with the life growing in her.

Was it really his baby?

"Hmm...that's better." Paige snuggled back against his ribs, the tantalizing feel of her skin sliding over his torso already making him fantasize about a third go-round. Her fingers drifted over the scar on his chest. "I think I should tell you that I know who fathered my baby."

Hollis stiffened reflexively, his heartbeat convulsing in wary palpitations. Had she known all along who he was? Why wasn't she leaping out of the bed and throwing things at him? He stroked her hair with a trembling hand. "Y-you do?"

"Mmm-hmm. I had my suspicions, but I didn't want to say anything to you until I was sure."

Hollis rose up on his elbow so he could see her

face and strained to keep his own expression neutral. "Are you saying your memory has come back?"

She shook her head. "Not exactly. Just two brief flashes—more like glimpses of a man. I didn't know who he was until I went down to the lobby to pick up the photo of Hollis Fenton I asked his secretary to send over."

"And you recognized him from his photo?"

"Yes. I feel very awkward saying this to you, but I know that I slept with him and that I cared about him. It's not so much memories as gut intuition—just as I suspected when we met with Noreen that she knew me on more than a professional basis. I had the hotel print off a copy of the bill that Pacific Gateway Shipping paid for and I think the local calls listed on it will confirm that I had a personal relationship with him."

Blood beat a gale-force tattoo in Hollis's ears. In the same breath where she'd informed him he was going to be a father, she'd also told him she cared so much about him that she'd jumped into bed with someone else as soon as she'd learned he was dead. He felt thoroughly disgruntled even though he *was* the someone else. "You don't have any doubts?"

"No. I—" Her face flushed. "In the memory fragment we were, I mean, it was nighttime and he was in bed and—"

"That memorable, huh?"

"Not *that!* I was going to say that even though it was obviously dark, I could make out a distinctive rope design on the quilt. I wonder if Noreen might be able to arrange for me to see his bedroom if they haven't already disposed of his belongings—"

The shrill ring of the phone interrupted their conversation. Hollis left Paige in the bed and stalked across the room to grab the phone, feeling like strangling someone. She remembered his decor, but not him. ''Yes,'' he barked.

''It's Noreen. I'm afraid I've got some upsetting news. My home was broken into this morning while I was out having my hair done. I thought you'd want to know that the only things missing are Paige's laptop and her briefcase.''

Hollis nearly dropped the phone. Someone had obviously stolen Paige's laptop and her briefcase for the same reason they wanted to kill her before she regained her memory. They were afraid she knew something. Thank God he had a copy of her file hidden in the lining of his suitcase. Maybe there was something in it he'd overlooked.

Chapter Ten

"Why did Noreen insist on meeting us here?" Paige asked, her gaze drawn to the memorial wreath flanking a brass plaque hung on the marble lobby wall of the Pacific Gateway Shipping building.

"I don't know," Matt grumbled in a low tone, frowning as he followed her gaze. "I'm just following orders. And I think you should, too, if you want a guided tour of Hollis Fenton's bedroom."

Paige glanced at him sharply as he gave their names to the security guard. Was that a note of jealousy she heard in Matt's voice? Something had definitely changed between them since she'd told him who'd fathered her baby. Maybe he was upset that she seemed to be holding information back from him. Or maybe things had just changed because they'd made love.

She shivered with pleasure just thinking about it.

Of course, she told herself brusquely, her escape from injury this morning was proof that deep down beneath the uncertainty created by her amnesia she was still the independent woman she'd always been and she could cope just fine on her own. With or without Matt, she'd figure out a way to take care of a baby. Millions of single women did it all the time and Paige was sure at some point they all felt as scared at the prospect as she did.

The security guard escorted them into the elevator, then ushered them to a reception area on another floor. Constructed of a pale wood, the receptionist's desk curved like the prow of a ship and served as a frame for a massive relief carving of a fleet of ships traversing an agitated sea. It was a magnificent work of art. As were the oil and watercolor seascapes tastefully positioned on the sky blue walls above a grouping of sleek, navy leather chairs.

Paige cast an appreciative eye at the furnishings, willing herself to remember something as they were escorted down a corridor past offices with those same pale wood doors carved with nautical themes. At the end of the corridor was a pair of double doors adorned with a killer whale. Paige suddenly felt short of breath. Perspiration beaded on her forehead with every step that brought her closer to that door. Though the brass nameplate indicated they were being shown to Evelyn Hollis-Styles's office, the distinction of the double doors could only mean this was the president's office; that it had once been Hollis's office.

Courage, she reminded herself running her fingers over the flank of the killer whale as she stepped into the room. Her eyes darted immediately to the incredible view of the shrouded North Shore mountains rising steeply across the inlet. The gray waters of the inlet looked as agitated as the sea in the carving on the receptionist's desk.

Paige couldn't explain it, but something felt wrong as she took in the cream tapestry walls, the rich tex-

tures of the upholstered furniture and the pervasive
scent of the huge bouquet of roses and gladioli that
dominated a Queen Anne library table, uncomfortably aware of Matt's intensely blue eyes on her as
she did so.

"Mrs. Muir will be joining you shortly," the guard
said, backing out of the room and closing the door.

Paige took a deep breath, determined not to hide
anything more from Matt about her awakening memories. "I think this was his office," she blurted out.

Matt tilted his head to one side, his expression
closed as he shifted his gaze and appeared to study
the open calendar on Evelyn Hollis-Styles's elegant
desk. "How do you know?"

"Physiological responses. My palms are damp, my
heart's pounding like crazy and my knees abandoned
me when the guard started leading us down the corridor."

Paige's heart pounded for another reason when
Matt ran a hand wearily over his face. "Worse than
that," she said haltingly, "I have the feeling something is wrong." It wasn't her imagination, he was
displeased about her candor. She stepped toward him
wanting to ford the gulf that seemed to be rapidly
expanding between them. Why wouldn't he look at
her? What was so fascinating about the damn desk?
"I'm sorry if my comments about Hollis make you
uncomfortable. I was just trying to be honest with
you—"

He turned with a groan and laid a finger on her
lips. "Don't apologize. I'm the one who's sorry. I
want you to be honest with me, Paige. Without trust,
we don't have anything." For a breathless second
Paige hoped he would throw caution and propriety to

the wind and kiss her senseless until the amity between them was restored. "Try to focus on what you feel is wrong—"

He broke off as the door opened behind them, his hands dropping to his sides.

Hollis's irritation at the interruption multiplied to full-blown apprehension when he saw who accompanied Noreen: his Uncle Luther and Aunt Evelyn. Was this whole mess going to blow up in his face, here and now?

At least he derived some pleasure from seeing Aunt Evelyn's double chin waggle when her jaw hinged open at the sight of him. But she quickly composed herself, pressing her thin red lips together in their familiar line of disapproval and refused to meet his gaze.

No doubt she was worried he wanted his office back. Hollis noticed she hadn't wasted any time redecorating the place to her tastes, even though she knew full well he wasn't dead. He'd probably never get the smell of her flowers and perfume out of here.

"Paige Roberts, Matt Darby," Noreen said briskly with a mutinous gleam in her eyes as she addressed him under his alias, "I'd like to introduce you to Luther Hollis and his sister, Evelyn Hollis-Styles. They were Mr. Fenton's uncle and aunt."

Hollis frowned, suspecting his aunt and uncle were up to something with his little charade. His Uncle Luther instantly took charge, his trademark forcefulness ringing in his gravelly voice. "Ms. Roberts. Mr. Darby. I'm sorry to meet you under such circumstances."

With a quiver of concern, Matt noticed his uncle seemed noticeably frailer than he had a month ago.

The white in his thick sandy hair seemed more predominant. And the navy blazer he wore over a lemon knit polo shirt didn't conceal a sag in the once proud, unbreakable line of his shoulders.

Aunt Evelyn didn't bother with pleasantries. She looked down her haughty nose at Paige, her hazel eyes sharp with suspicion. "Ms. Roberts. Noreen here leads us to believe that you had a relationship of an intimate nature with Hollis."

Hollis gritted his teeth and groaned inwardly. He should have known Noreen might do something like this.

Noreen, at least, had the decency to flush for meddling. "Do forgive me, Ms. Roberts. Under the circumstances, I felt it imperative that Mr. Hollis and Mrs. Hollis-Styles be informed of the er…situation."

Paige lifted her chin a notch, her eyes gleaming with a defensive light. "It's quite all right, Noreen. I understand you were only doing what you thought best."

"For crying out loud, Ev," Luther groused. "I thought we agreed that I would handle this."

"Oh, Luther, I'm not going to allow this hussy to waltz into our lives and sully Hollis's name and reputation. Especially when he's not able to defend himself."

Hollis nearly snorted in disbelief at the idea of his aunt viewing herself as a guardian of his reputation.

"Just how far along are you?" Evelyn demanded.

"I beg your pardon?" Paige set her lips.

They knew about the baby! Hollis seriously considered firing Noreen.

"I know what your game is and if you think—"

"Ev, that's enough!" Luther roared. "I think we

ought to let Ms. Roberts get a word in edgewise. Are we to understand that you've recovered from your amnesia?''

Paige shook her head and stood her ground like a lioness. ''Unfortunately, no. I'm not certain what Noreen has told you, but there's a considerable gap in my memory which I'm trying to reconstruct. I'm following the paper trail I have of my trip and a few memory fragments that have surfaced. I'm still hoping I'll eventually recover my memory completely. But what I've recovered so far leaves me little doubt I had a close relationship with Hollis Fenton—especially after I saw his picture this morning.''

Luther shot Hollis a probing glance, then gave Paige a steely survey from head to toe. ''Noreen suspects you're pregnant. Is that true?''

''Yes.''

Luther frowned. ''Are you implying Hollis is the father?''

Paige's hands settled protectively over her belly. ''I know he is.''

''For heaven's sake, Luther,'' Evelyn hissed. ''Ask her how many men she's seen in the last few months.''

Hollis was sorely tempted to point out that his aunt was in no position to throw stones at Paige's choice of companions. Not when he'd seen on her calendar a few minutes ago when he and Paige were alone in the office that his aunt had as poor taste in men as Hollis's mother had. Evelyn had a dinner with his father-in-law penciled in on Monday.

''I can't speak for Ms. Roberts,'' Hollis said sharply, glaring at his aunt, ''but I find this conversation insulting. Perhaps we should be leaving.''

Paige laid a hand on his forearm. "No, Matt, it's okay. They have a right to know about the baby. And I don't have anything to hide."

"Just precisely what is your intention regarding the child?" Luther went on. "Are you considering an abortion?"

A shower of angry sparks shot from Paige's eyes. "That's not a choice I'm willing to entertain. Hollis gave me this baby and I'm going to do my best to raise it in a loving environment."

Luther exchanged a conspiratorial glance with his sister. Hollis knew that look. An ax was about to fall.

"Hollis's death has been a shock to all of us," his uncle replied solemnly. "He was not fond of scandal. He had quite enough of it after his wife's unfortunate death and I think the circumstances of his father's leaving hurt him very deeply. I can only guess how he would feel to know that news of an illegitimate offspring would be broadcast through the media. But I can't imagine him turning his back on his child either. So, this is what we propose. We are willing to offer you an immediate settlement now in exchange for your silence about the baby. Though we are sympathetic with your desire to recover your memory, we can't have you causing a scandal."

He paused for dramatic effect, pulling a check out of the breast pocket of his blazer. "This is a cashier's check for one hundred thousand dollars. *After* a paternity test is conducted following the child's live birth, we'll enter into negotiations for child support."

Paige eyed the check with disdain that made Hollis's chest swell with pride. "Thank you, Mr. Hollis, but in all good conscience, I can't accept your terms or your offer. My baby has a right to know who his father was and the circumstances of his conception, as do my parents, my friends and Hollis's family. I'm very sorry that you view this pregnancy as a potentially embarrassing incident, but I know in my heart that I must have genuinely cared about your nephew. And I won't allow you to taint our relationship or our baby with your bribe money. I had hoped you might derive comfort in knowing that part of your nephew would still live on.'' Paige squared her shoulders and jutted her chin up another notch. ''And just so there's no misunderstanding, although your offer of support is very generous, it is neither wanted, nor needed. I'm entirely capable of meeting this baby's emotional and material needs. However, I'm willing to be very generous with visitation if you change your mind and wish this baby to be part of your family.''

Her speech brought an unfamiliar moisture to Hollis's eyes. He wasn't sure when he'd ever seen his uncle and aunt so flabbergasted.

''You don't want money?'' Luther reiterated as if he didn't know what to do with the check he still held in his hand.

''No. But I do want something.''

Aunt Evelyn arched a well-plucked brow. ''Ah, here it comes, Luther. The counteroffer.''

Paige sighed and Hollis would have given anything to be a party to her thoughts. ''I simply want your cooperation in seeing Hollis's abductors caught and punished. I presume Noreen has informed you that my friend's husband, Claude, was the first victim.''

''Yes, she has,'' Luther admitted.

Paige explained the goal of her research into the kidnappings. ''It may seem like a long shot, but these articles may show us commonalities in how the kidnappers think and why they selected each victim.''

Evelyn sniffed. ''It seems to me you're the common factor in the kidnappings. You show up to interview Hollis and suddenly he becomes a victim. There were only four people who knew we'd contacted the police—Luther, me, Noreen and you. Noreen's loyalty to this family is beyond question.''

Paige recoiled as if she'd been slapped. ''Me?''

Hollis peered at Paige closely, his breath feeling like lead in his lungs. He could feel his aunt and uncle observing his reaction, too. Trust Aunt Evelyn to get to the gritty core of any subject.

Evelyn nodded. ''And you insisted on meeting Hollis in the lobby the morning of the explosion. Hollis invited you to come to the house, but you refused. For all we know, you were involved in the kidnapping from the start. You were probably behind the theft of Sandford's cellular phone, too. Do you have any idea how horrified we all felt when the police took him in for questioning? He'd reported the phone stolen two months earlier.''

''I won't dignify that with a response.''

''And you don't have to either,'' Luther declared. ''If Hollis trusted you, we do, too. Evelyn is very upset. She viewed Hollis as a personal thorn in her side and is outraged that someone has removed that amusement from her life, much less had the gall to attempt to pin the blame on her son. Though she tried hard to hide it, in her own way, she was very fond of our sister's only child.''

Evelyn blinked rapidly, her eyes noticeably damp. ''His mother and I were twins, though not identical. We argued over everything when we were younger—

clothes, boys, privileges, who was prettier, smarter. But let Luther try to lord his superiority over us and we rallied together against him. We considered it our duty to take his ego down a peg or two. Oh, we've had some chaotic times in this family, but nothing to quite equal this. Of course, Hollis always ended up in the limelight, even though he never wanted it— just like his mother.'' She forced a quavering smile as her eyes darted from Paige to Hollis, lingering just a fraction of a second longer on Hollis. ''It's true what they say. Sometimes you don't realize how much people mean to you until they're gone.''

Hollis shifted uncomfortably, confused by his aunt's behavior that seemed far too genuine to be an act. Of course, that hadn't stopped her from assuming his title and redecorating his office.

''There, there, Ev,'' Luther mumbled, awkwardly patting her shoulder. ''Pull yourself together. We need to be strong.'' He turned to Paige. ''Ms. Roberts, we'll give you whatever assistance you require in your research on two conditions. One, that I be kept informed of the progress at all times, and, two, that you allow us to provide you with secure accommodations during your stay. I'm sure the hotel is very comfortable, but I would never forgive myself if something happened to you or the baby. I pulled a few strings and I have a condo standing by—it's fully furnished and stocked with groceries. No one could possibly know you're there and it has a state-of-the-art security system.''

''Is this your way of preventing me from sullying your nephew's reputation? By keeping me out of sight?'' Paige asked with well-warranted suspicion.

''On the contrary, you've already proven yourself

to be a woman of strong ethics. I'm just not willing to take any more chances with my nephew's flesh and blood. These people have brutally killed twice, but I'll be damned if I'll let them get away with what they've done to my family.''

Paige folded her arms across her chest. ''I'd like to discuss it with Matt privately if you don't mind.''

''Of course. We'll give you a few moments.''

Hollis frowned, completely befuddled by this unexpected show of family support as his aunt, uncle and secretary filed out into the hall, closing the door behind them. That was very odd indeed. Were they feeling guilty for disobeying the kidnappers instructions? He was half-tempted to yank the door open to see whether they would stoop to eavesdrop on his conversation with Paige—though, knowing his family, chances were they already had a listening device secreted somewhere. Or maybe, just once, he could give them the benefit of the doubt and let himself believe they loved him—just as he wanted to let himself believe that Paige cared about him whether he was Matt Darby or Hollis Fenton.

''What do you think, Matt?''

''I think you handled them with extraordinary aplomb.''

To his complete distraction, a delicate rosy-pink tone crept over her jaw to shade her cheeks, reminding him of how flushed her skin looked after a vigorous round of lovemaking. ''I meant about the condo.''

Hollis massaged his forehead. ''There's no denying they have connections and information that could come in very useful.''

"It would be easier to accept his offer if I didn't feel as if he were trying to control me."

Hollis laughed. "For men like Luther Hollis, life is all about power and control." He clasped her hand and kissed the tip of her nose. "You did your fair share of trying to exert control, too. I do agree with Luther, however, that your safety is of paramount importance. I'd rather meet with Noreen in a covert, secure environment than have us traipsing in and out of public hotels and restaurants where we don't know who's watching. I'll bet if we insist, Luther could wave his magic wand and get us safely installed in that condo without anyone being the wiser—unless, of course, that gut instinct you were experiencing before they walked into the room was about them. Did something about them feel wrong—like you couldn't trust them?"

"I'm not sure they trust each other. What a family!" Paige's brow wrinkled in concentration, then she sighed in frustration. "I don't know, Matt. The feeling is gone now. Maybe it's tied in somehow with the inconsistencies we discussed in Hollis Fenton's kidnapping after we met with Noreen, though she didn't mention anything about a stolen cell phone. It's pretty creepy that the phone was stolen from Evelyn's son. I'll try reaching Professor Zbarsky again to ask what his take is on all this. It's odd, he said he'd be at his cottage. Maybe he's spending a lot of time fishing and isn't bothering to check his answering machine at home."

She stepped in front of the window and stared out at the inclement weather outside. "At least being here makes me feel closer to Hollis. His family knew him better than anyone. Whether I like it or not, the most viable recourse is to trust them and accept their hospitality.''

Hollis sighed in resignation, agreeing with her completely.

But that didn't stop him from demanding a private word with his uncle twenty minutes later when Paige's need for a bathroom break interrupted a group discussion about the security arrangements to ensure their safety.

''I don't appreciate being manipulated like this,'' Hollis flatly informed his uncle.

''You don't appreciate being manipulated?'' Luther roared, his face reddening. ''I've been half out of my mind worrying about you. Just what the hell do you think you're doing? You're supposed to be recuperating in Prince Edward Island, not traipsing around the country with a woman you hardly know, whose belongings were stolen from Noreen's home this morning. I'd like to know why I was never informed of these belongings in the first place.''

''Because it was my personal business.''

''Well, as long as I'm still breathing, you're my personal business and I promised your mother I'd always treat you like a son. I want to know what was stolen.''

Hollis stared at him, reluctant to acknowledge that despite his uncle's claim, he'd always felt like an outsider in their midst. ''You mean Noreen didn't tell you?''

''No, and by the way, I'm deducting the cost of a new security system for her home and temporary accommodations until this situation blows over from your salary.''

Hollis grudgingly explained what information was

in Paige's laptop and her files. "Some of the information appeared damaging. I was worried the police would arrest her if they found it. Sergeant Thurlo was suspicious enough of her as it was. But I know she wasn't involved. Someone broke into her home and tried to attack her. They used a knife just like the one the kidnappers left me to cut myself free."

Luther turned a sharp glare upon him—the glare that warned employees and business associates he knew he wasn't being given the straight goods. "What do you think this theft signifies?"

"That she knows more than she realizes about the kidnappings. With time, and luck, she may remember yet." He shrugged his shoulders, feeling a keen sense of disappointment. "I suppose all that other stuff you said in there was just for show."

"No, that my boy, was the damn truth. We're your family and we'll stand behind you one hundred percent. We've all done everything we can to convince the world you're dead. I can understand why you would risk your life for a woman you obviously care about, but why would you take the risk of revealing yourself to Will Harper?"

Hollis's jaw hardened. "Why would you risk letting the police insert a tracking device in the bag along with the ransom?"

His uncle's face turned ashen. "Because someone dared to put a member of my family at risk and I wasn't going to let the bastards get away with it or let them put anyone else through the same hell we've suffered." He looped a frail arm around Hollis's shoulders. "I'll regret that decision to my dying day. Please let me advise Sergeant Thurlo how you've been hiding out these last few weeks. You two might be safer under police protection.''

Hollis shook his head. ''No. It's my life and my decision. Besides, I think Paige will bolt if we bring the police in now. She didn't want to call them after she was attacked in her home or after the other attacks. I'm not sure whether it's because she's embarrassed she has amnesia or simply feels she lacks credibility, but I'd rather she approach them when she's ready and has something to tell them. Whether or not these articles lead to anything concrete that will help the police, at least her pursuit of them has helped her figure out that she had a relationship with me.''

Luther sighed. ''All right, son, I'll respect your decision.'' To Hollis's surprise, his uncle hugged him. Hard. ''Be safe.''

THEY ARRIVED BACK to the meeting place on schedule, the grim set of their lips an indication of the success of their mission.

''I suspect all did not go as planned,'' their leader remarked, perturbed by the possibility of yet one more delay.

''Only partially.'' A booted foot kicked a black metal wastebasket. ''That bitch has more lives than a cat. But we found this at the secretary's house. I guess she was holding it for her.'' A file folder and a zippered canvas case that the leader presumed held a computer, were pulled out of a large knapsack and set on the table.

He flipped open the file and thumbed through the pages. The contents made him curse under his breath. He eased back in the chair, thinking of options and loose ends. They wouldn't truly be safe until Paige Roberts was silenced. His gaze settled on his companions. ''Her luck runs out today. No more excuses. Resume your surveillance at her hotel. Do whatever you have to do as long as she and her boyfriend meet with an unfortunate accident.''

Chapter Eleven

Being hunched down in the back of a cleaning van as it whisked away from the service entrance of the Pacific Gateway Shipping building was not Paige's preferred way to travel, but Paige figured she had no other choice but to go along for the ride.

She dug her nails into Matt's arm as the van made yet another turn to elude potential followers. If the mounting nausea wasn't discomforting enough, she had an urgent need to use the ladies' room.

The van turned into an enclosed parking garage of the Pan Pacific Hotel. The rear doors were jerked open and Jax Phillips, the VIP security consultant whom Luther Hollis relied upon for personal protection, hustled them toward a white limousine with tinted windows.

Paige sank gratefully into the pristine leather seat and decided no one would appreciate a rest stop. She and Matt had reluctantly surrendered their hotel key so their belongings could be transported separately to their new location. At least they had their research records with them so she didn't have to worry about them being lost.

Jax Phillips spoke to them from the front passenger

seat as the limo pulled out into the street. "It shouldn't be long now. Fifteen minutes max if there's no traffic over the bridge."

Paige stifled a groan.

"You don't look happy." Matt wrapped an arm around her shoulders and tucked a strand of hair behind her ear. "What's the matter, I thought you appreciated a life of luxury?" he gestured to the well-appointed interior of the limo.

"Not at the moment. I'm getting car sick and I have to go to the bathroom."

"But you just went before we left—"

"Tell that to the baby."

To her amusement, he leaned down and addressed her stomach. "Hey, kid, your timing leaves a bit to be desired."

Paige laughed at his understatement.

Matt's eyes smoldered with warmth. "That's what you needed, a distraction. And I'm the right man for the job."

She sobered at his words. Is that what he thought he was to her—a temporary distraction? A lump formed in her throat when she realized she wanted him to be so much more.

He circled her thumb with his thumb and forefinger, tugging on it gently. "Which gives me an idea. Have you ever made love in a limo?"

"What—here?" Her eyes darted anxiously toward the privacy panel separating them from the driver and the security consultant, one of whom might feel obliged to report such activity to Luther Hollis.

Matt's warm breath fanned her ear like a sultry breeze. "Don't worry about them. They won't see anything but me whispering in your ear."

Lured into reluctant acquiescence, Paige listened in rapt attention as Matt's silken-toned discourse roused her senses into a sensuous fury. The gliding motion of his fingers over her thumb illustrated his description in exquisite detail. Paige caught her breath at the volley of tingling sensations rippling over her skin and the moist heat gathering to welcome him into her body. She was vaguely aware of their passage across the elegant silver span of the Lions Gate Bridge and the towering trees that lined the road which led them to the condo situated on the Capilano River.

She shuddered in near ecstasy as Matt's tongue flicked into her ear. "We're here, sweetheart."

"What?" Paige blinked, trying to get a fix on their surroundings. Obviously, his distraction tactics had been successful, she thought ruefully. The limo had stopped outside a security gate painted a sand color that blended with the high fieldstone wall surrounding the development. Phillips passed the driver a key card to open the gate. The condos had a definite West Coast air with huge windows to let in light and stained cedar siding. They were set amidst landscaping that Audrey would have adored. Streams, reflective ponds, pathways and beds of brilliantly-hued flowers enhanced velvet green oases of lawn.

Paige tried not to hop from one foot to the other as Phillips opened the door and gave them keys to the condo and the car in the garage, plus a key card to the gate. She gave him a smile of thanks and ducked into the luxuriously appointed guest bath.

When she emerged a few moments later, she found Matt alone in the marble-tiled living room examining a Robert Bateman painting hanging over the fireplace. The vaulted ceiling of the space, its ecru painted walls and the glass-topped tables enhanced, rather than diminished the overpowering impact Matt had on her. Paige couldn't take her eyes off him, still feeling the mesmerizing effects of the images he'd described to her in such intimate detail in the limo.

She cleared her throat. "This is a nice prison. Is it equipped with a phone? Maybe I'll catch Professor Zbarsky frying fish for his dinner."

Matt turned. The wolfish grin that tugged at his mouth as their eyes met made her feel desired and terribly vulnerable all at the same time. "There's a portable phone on the table behind the sofa. I'll get it for you."

Paige was aware of his every movement as she dug into her purse for the professor's business card. She let the phone ring a dozen times at his cottage. Then she left a message and her phone number at the condo on the answering machine at his home number. "Still no response." She set the phone down on the coffee table and wet her lips nervously as her gaze climbed over Matt's lean hips and up the rigid contours of his chest, to his face. "What, uh, do you suggest we do now?"

His eyes were blunt with suggestion. "I want to finish what we started earlier. How 'bout you?"

Paige reached for him with trembling fingers, bracing herself for the emotional onslaught of his kiss. As far as she was concerned, she didn't want what they'd started to ever end.

HOLLIS WAITED UNTIL he was sure Paige was deeply asleep before he recovered the file from the lining of his suitcase. If his uncle had searched his bags before he'd delivered them, Hollis couldn't tell. Part of him desperately wanted to believe that the loving words his aunt and uncle had spoken today were true, but he wasn't prepared to risk Paige's safety if he was wrong. The knife Paige's attacker had left behind was still secreted in one of his shoes. Hollis took Paige's file into the kitchen and went over the pages word by word, hoping something significant would leap out at him. The cryptic list he'd once thought so suspicious was obviously the notes Paige had taken during her interview with Susan Platham-Burke. There were newspaper and magazine articles about other executives that she'd marked, ''To interview, if possible.'' He found his own name circled in an article about his uncle in *Fortune Magazine* dated seven months ago. He flipped through the interview notes Noreen had printed off of a diskette found in Paige's briefcase. His own initial interview with Paige was there in black and white, minus his cocky endeavors to flirt with her. Hollis felt as if he'd aged ten years since that day.

Being physically close to Paige again was a double-edged blade of pain and peace. God help him, he loved her. But he wanted her and the baby in Hollis Fenton's life, not Matt Darby's. He blinked his dry eyes. It would be a relief to be rid of these infernal contact lenses and all the lies. He'd consider it a blessing never to stare at himself in the mirror again, tweezers in hand, plucking rogue blond hairs from his eyebrows.

WITH THE HOPE that they might soon find one or more articles about each victim that singled them out as potential targets to the kidnappers, Paige handed Matt a highlighter and explained that they would scan the articles and mark any personal information they contained. "We'll read the pertinent parts out loud as we highlight so Noreen can add the information, the source and the date to the lists I've been compiling from the articles we've already gathered. Pay close attention to the dates of the articles. Each kidnapping probably took weeks of planning. They needed time to learn the victim's schedule, find a place to hold them hostage and devise a drop for the ransom."

They started on Claude Belanger's pile of clippings since he was the first victim. Paige suggested they begin by reading any articles that appeared in *The Globe and Mail* since the newspaper was national in scope and readily available in newsstands across the country, then move on to articles that were gleaned from local papers. The kidnappers might have worked in the same way—finding a prospective name in the national business paper, then doing further research in the newspapers of the victim's home city.

Her hopes that they'd find an article in *The Globe and Mail* that pinpointed Claude as an obvious target were soon dashed. All they found were a couple of employee appointment notices that were about people placed in key management positions in Claude's translation service company. Claude was just listed as the president announcing their appointment.

Paige told Matt to toss the articles.

They moved on to the other papers. Claude's company had received press in Ottawa, Moncton, and Toronto where it had operational divisions. In Montreal, his family and their activities were frequently mentioned in *The Gazette*. Paige and Matt read out snatches as they found them. Noreen diligently wrote them down.

Then they tackled Susan Platham-Burke's piles. Fortunately, Miss Platham-Burke and the clipping service she'd hired had been incredibly thorough. But Matt found an appointment notice in *The Globe and Mail* that was not already on the list. Speculation rose in his voice as he quoted part of the article, "'As part of a Valentine campaign, Miss Platham-Burke, newly appointed national spokesperson for the Our Hearts are for Children Organization, is encouraging businesses to open their corporate wallets and fund local programs to benefit children who may one day be their future employees...' It goes on to describe her family and its corporate commitment to charities, and it lists her position as director of public relations. What's more, the article appeared in February—six months before her abduction."

"Too bad we didn't find an article like that about Claude in *The Globe and Mail*," Paige said wistfully, sifting through a number of press releases about the Platham-Burke family's agricultural products company, in which Miss Platham-Burke was listed as a spokesperson. "That article's like waving a red flag in front of a bull. Maybe the result of this search will show us the kidnappers selected their victims from various sources."

"Or they selected a city at random, moved in and studied the local media for potential targets," Matt said. "Remember, Will Harper was convinced his name was brought to the kidnappers' attention because he was profiled in a local business magazine?"

Paige cautioned herself against reaching any conclusions too soon. Will Harper was next on their agenda. The pile on the floor grew as they discarded articles she had already seen and an employee appointment notice in *The Globe and Mail* for last October in which Harper, as President and CEO of the real estate investment corporation, announced the hiring of an assistant vice-president of acquisitions. The article wasn't about Harper per se, but her eyes bulged when she read the company was a subsidiary of HarpCor and had assets of several hundred million. She highlighted the information and read it out to Noreen.

When Paige could no longer ignore her growling stomach, they took a break to whip up mushroom omelets and a garden salad for dinner. Further fortified with a slice of the chocolate cake they'd found in the freezer, they resumed working.

Paige was most curious about Ellen Cummings, the mother of five, who was president of a home health care company in her family's international group of human resources companies. The Halifax papers carried a number of articles about her car accident—she'd been struck head-on by a drunk driver—and her recovery. There were also other articles about the growing need for supplementary health care in times of medical cutbacks and hospital closures.

"There's nothing interesting in *The Globe and Mail* on her," Matt said. "A few news bulletins, a letter to the editor from last year and an appointment ad for a new general manager of Cummings Health Services in Vancouver. So much for my theory that all these executives would be featured in appointment announcements."

Paige blinked. "What did you say?"

"I said it was too much to hope for an obvious link—"

"You're right. These people are smart. It would have to be something obscure." Like *The Globe and Mail* employee announcements they'd been tossing away as unimportant....except that she'd kept one because it had mentioned HarpCo's assets. Adrenaline flowed through her like a rising tide as a possibility took shape in her mind. "What's the date on that announcement for the general manager's position for Cummings Health Services?"

"January twelfth of this year."

"Just after Harper's kidnapping and three months before Ellen Cummings's kidnapping when they would be searching for their next victim." Paige skimmed the articles piled on the table. "Quick, where's that appointment notice I read to you a few minutes ago with all the information about Harper's company on it?"

Noreen efficiently produced the clipping as though out of thin air. "Here it is. It's dated October sixth."

"That's two months before Harper's kidnapping," Paige said, thinking out loud. Was this only conjecture or were they on to something? "Matt, weren't there some announcements with Claude Belanger's name on them?"

"Yeah, two. But you told me to throw them away."

Oh no! Paige looked at the articles mounded on the plush beige carpet at the base of the glass table and dropped to her knees. "No, problem. We'll find them. Noreen, you look through Hollis Fenton's pile to see if he was mentioned in one of these announcements and pull out that piece we saw on Susan Platham-Burke's involvement in the Valentine's Day campaign.''

Matt helped her weed through the discarded articles. Paige didn't take time to be tidy. Papers flew in the air around them. "Here's one," she breathed, her heart thundering. Disappointment crested hard in her as she noted the date. "Darn. It's dated a week before Claude's kidnapping. That's not nearly enough time to plan a kidnapping.''

Matt dangled a piece of paper under her nose. "How does five months sound? This one's dated the third week of January. It appeared a couple weeks before the article about Susan Platham-Burke.''

Paige grasped the paper with trembling fingers. "If we've got a clipping with Hollis Fenton's name on it, I think we have a workable theory. Noreen?''

Suspense stretched taut as a rubber band into the silence. "Oh, my goodness," Noreen whispered. "There is one, though it's twenty months old. Still, that's two months before the January appointment notice mentioning Claude Belanger's name.''

"Which illustrates just how long they've been planning the kidnappings.'' Paige's knees buckled and she shared a joyful smile with Matt as his arm slipped tightly around her waist.

He kissed her brow. "You did it, sweetheart. Now that we know how the victims are selected we can figure out who their next target will be and get the police involved. Maybe the police can catch the kidnappers in the act.''

"We did it," she corrected him, caressing his jaw until she noticed Noreen was frowning at them. Paige discreetly disentangled herself from Matt's embrace out of respect for Noreen's feelings.

Noreen cleared her throat. "Though why was Hollis the fifth victim and not the second or third?" she asked.

Paige sat down at the table. "I can think of a couple of reasons. One, the kidnappers have proven themselves to be very smart. If Hollis was one of the first three victims, there was a risk the police might make the connection as to how they were finding their victims. So it made good sense to save him as a reserve card. Plus, they probably considered him expendable since he didn't have a spouse and children. It's just as Professor Zbarsky explained. The victims were deliberately picked for maximum emotional appeal. They killed Claude, who had a wife and family, to show they meant business and it worked like a charm with the next three victims. The theft of the cell phone two months prior to Hollis's kidnapping suggests they planned to make another example out of him as a corporate crown prince, to keep the families of their future victims from getting ideas about calling in the police."

Paige pointed at an article Noreen had given her about Christine Fenton's suicide. "It's possible his wife's suicide gave Hollis added emotional appeal, though the media didn't really play it up in their reports on Hollis's kidnapping." She glanced at Noreen, unable to restrain her curiosity about Hollis's first wife. "Did Christine really abduct a baby from a hospital?"

"I'm afraid so. She was a lovely girl with a sensitive soul. Very energetic, but highly strung and prone to moods. Hollis didn't learn until after they were married that she suffered from a manic-depressive illness. As long as she took her medication she was fine, but the problem with that sort of illness is the patient tends to equate taking medication with being sick. Once the medication begins to make them feel better, they believe they are well and stop taking the medication. Christine desperately wanted to start a family. Hollis loved her dearly but he was very concerned about her ability to care for a baby. She decided if he wouldn't let her get pregnant, she'd find a baby any way she could and prove to him she could be a good mother. She was very mixed up. I think she meant to return the baby, but the infant's parents were terribly traumatized." Noreen lowered her gaze to the table as if reliving those past events in her mind's eye. "I don't think Hollis ever forgave himself for her death, or her father-in-law for taking her out of the hospital. But that's all ancient history now."

Noreen let out a shaky sigh and Paige squeezed the older woman's hand in compassion. "Hollis's baby is going to need a godmother. Are you interested in applying for the position?"

Noreen gave Paige a wavering smile, her eyes suspiciously moist. "Indeed I am. Thank you, dear. And thank you for possessing the fortitude to get to the root of this evil and find the truth. I must admit that business about the different hoods truly had me concerned. I was terribly worried the Hollis family squabbles had finally resulted in bloodshed. I couldn't figure out how else the kidnappers learned my unlisted phone number..."

"Matt and I had similar concerns," Paige admitted, exchanging a warm, conspiratorial smile with Matt, who seemed a little damp-eyed himself. "But the important thing now is to put our theory to the test. The kidnappers may have already selected their next victim and are plotting his or her abduction. Let's see if we can second-guess them. If it works, we'll contact the police ASAP and show them what we've got.''

Chapter Twelve

They didn't hear him when he let himself in the house. Snores told him they were still asleep. He walked into the living room where one of his men was curled onto the sagging couch. Empty pizza boxes and the wrappings and soggy paper cups from fast-food restaurants covered a cheap plastic patio table.

His foot accidentally knocked over a beer bottle on the worn braided rug and the smell of stale beer invaded his nostrils along with the ripe odors of cheese and pepperoni. Pigs. They never cleaned up after themselves, much less opened a window.

He picked up the brown Stetson perched on the lid of a pizza box and dropped it over the indelicate view of its owner's gaping mouth and crooked teeth. He got an instant reaction.

"Hey, what the—? Oh, it's you boss."

"Have you found her yet?"

"No. It's like the bitch and her boyfriend vanished off the face of the earth."

"I'm in no mood for your excuses. What about Noreen Muir? Have you tried following her? She probably knows where they are."

"She hasn't been home or reported to her office in days."

"Damn. The break-in must have spooked her."

"The Hollis mansion is crawling with security. Could be they're all there."

"Wake the others. I've got an idea that might just work."

HOLLIS FELT CHILLS creep down his spine as he looked at the results of their intensive two-day search. The thought that someone's life might hang in the balance had kept them working feverishly. Noreen had supplied them with two computers, Dun & Bradstreet's *Canadian Key Business Directory,* a Canadian atlas and a CD-ROM containing the back issues of *The Globe and Mail.* They'd set to work, taking turns scanning the business announcements for likely prospects and researching the companies in the business directory and on the Internet to ensure they were divisions or subsidiaries of corporations primarily owned by family members. Since all five kidnappings took place in major urban centers, they ruled out isolated communities where the banks might have difficulty having funds for a ransom demand delivered in under two days.

They came up with three company presidents who fit the profile: two men and one woman.

A search of the newspaper archives in their cities of residence had yielded information about their marital statuses, families and personal interests. Even pictures.

It was frightening knowing what the future might hold in store for them. Hollis gripped Paige's hand as Noreen called Luther and gave him the news. He had to give Paige credit for seeing this through to the end and not giving up, even when she couldn't remember her relationship with him.

If there was one cloud obscuring the hope that his abductors would soon be caught and put away for a long time, it was that Paige hadn't progressed any further in recovering her memory. What if she never did?

Noreen hung up the phone. "Mr. Hollis wants us to sit tight. He insists he'll bring the police to us. They should be here in under an hour. I'll put a fresh pot of decaf coffee on."

Hollis stroked the back of Paige's hand with his thumb. He didn't think he'd ever tire of touching her or feeling her curled up against him in bed. He'd woken up in the middle of the night and reached for her and she'd melted into him, her body sweet and respondent. His heartbeat quickened at the memory. "Nervous?" he asked.

Her silver eyes were luminous. "Petrified that after all this we'll be too late. I'm sure you'd like to get back to your normal life, too, and your clients."

"It's a tough choice, returning to normal life or being your bodyguard."

Paige's gaze flickered to Noreen, who was rinsing dirty mugs in the kitchen sink. "You know, once we tell the police about this, you could return to Montreal. I feel bad about all the time you've given up for me. Assuming a kidnapping hasn't already occurred, it could be days or weeks or months before the next one. I can't monopolize your time like that. I should be safe enough here." She flushed. "Besides, as much as I've enjoyed your protection, it's occurred to me that it might be easier for my memory to resurface if I wasn't so distracted by our relationship…''

Hollis's eyes narrowed. He couldn't believe it, she was giving him the boot. Maybe she was right though… But he'd be damned if he gave her any space beyond a separate bedroom until he was certain she was completely safe. He squeezed her fingers. ''Let's see how things go with the police and we'll talk about it again in a few days, okay?''

She nodded.

Hollis sighed. At least he'd negotiated a few days' reprieve to decide what to do next.

PAIGE GATHERED HER courage as Luther Hollis introduced her to Sergeant Thurlo, the head of the task force investigating Hollis Fenton's abduction and murder. Sergeant Thurlo was a brute of a man, six feet four inches with shoulders like a gorilla and a receding hairline that mimicked the shape of the interlocking curves on a baseball. His pale green eyes reflected a distrust that set Paige on edge. He was accompanied by Detective Boyle, the officer Paige had contacted about her missing laptop and briefcase. Boyle was shorter, less brawny and looked as if he hadn't slept in weeks.

''Ms. Roberts,'' Sergeant Thurlo said. ''I've heard a lot about you in the last few days.''

Paige felt confused. Had Luther Hollis informed the police he was sheltering her? ''You have?''

''Yes. The Montreal police department was chagrined to report that you'd left town. We weren't sure where you'd disappeared to until Susan Platham-Burke contacted her local police and informed them you'd been to visit her. They contacted us. We had a feeling you'd eventually head in our direction with your bodyguard.'' Paige didn't like the way Thurlo examined Matt as if were some sort of criminal.

"I'm afraid I don't understand,'' she murmured.

"You're our only witness to the bombing. We've been keeping an eye on you.''

The idea made Paige's flesh crawl. "Where were the police when some jerk broke into my home and tried to attack me with a knife?''

Thurlo's head jerked up like a lizard suddenly aware prey was within reach. "What's this?''

Paige told the story.

"I've got the knife in my luggage,'' Matt added. "I put it in a plastic bag to protect any fingerprints. I'll get it.'' He hastened out of the room.

"Why didn't you report the attack to the Montreal police?'' Thurlo demanded.

"Because I didn't want to tell anyone about the explosion and my amnesia. I was afraid my report would be received with the same attitude I'm getting right now.''

"I'm sorry, Ms. Roberts. But it's difficult enough to do our jobs without the public taking it upon themselves to determine on their own what may or may not be of importance to us—'' Thurlo broke off as Matt returned to the living room and handed him the knife.

He swore softly under his breath. "I'd say this was a significant piece of evidence. Take a look, Detective.''

"What's so significant about it?'' Paige asked.

"Hollis Fenton's kidnappers gave him a knife just like this to cut himself free,'' the sergeant explained. "We'll get it down to the lab ASAP. Have you remembered anything about the explosion, Ms. Roberts? I was hoping we were called here because you wanted to make a statement.''

Paige shook her head. ''But I hope you'll be equally interested in the other information I have to offer you.''

''Tell him about the other attacks first, Paige,'' Matt said. ''They should know about them.''

Paige glared at him for being so helpful. But at least Thurlo tempered the tone of his questions and took notes, pressing her for a detailed description of the two different vehicles which had nearly struck her. Though he seemed composed, Paige could see a thick vein pulsing in his temple.

''I don't believe this,'' he said when she'd finished. ''These people are killers. They've tracked you across the country and tried to run you down on Saturday. That was five days ago. They could be anywhere by now. You should have contacted us immediately Ms. Roberts.''

Paige reined in her temper. And she was willing to concede the sergeant had a point, but that was water under the bridge. ''Well, you're here now. Mr. Hollis arranged this meeting because Matt, Noreen and I have a good idea where the kidnappers may be now, or where they'll be in the very near future. For all we know one or two were dispatched to take care of me and the others are planning their next abduction.''

She got a certain amount of satisfaction from watching Thurlo's expression change from anger to interest as she explained Professor Zbarsky's theory and how the interviews with the other victims had led them to searching the newspapers for press clippings about the victims.

Thurlo interrupted her. "I'm sorry to burst your balloon, but I'm afraid you folks have wasted your time. We've already been down this path in our investigation. Our crime profilers have established many of the same points you've made. It's not exactly earth-shattering news that they're using the newspapers to pinpoint their victims."

"Just hear us out," Matt said in a deadly tone. "Your department screwed up once and cost Hollis Fenton his life. I think Kyle Foster, Evan Smythe and Natasha Blais might appreciate your giving us a few more minutes of your time."

"Who the hell are they?"

"The next victims."

"How do you figure that?"

Paige told him precisely, showing him the dates of the appointment notices and how they gave the kidnappers a name, a city and a company to research.

"Can we take this with us?" Sergeant Thurlo asked. We'll see that you get a copy in case you come up with any more insights."

Which was as close to a compliment as Paige figured they'd get out of him. "Of course."

"I'd like to talk to Professor Zbarsky, too. Have you got his number?"

"I've got it memorized. He must have been called out of town on an emergency. I keep getting his answering machine and there's no answer at his cottage. I tried calling him again before you got here." She recited both phone numbers.

"Thanks for coming to us with this. It could be the break we've been hoping for." Thurlo smiled, a genuine smile that made him look almost human, and as exhausted as Detective Boyle. "We'll keep in touch. And stay under wraps. There have been enough victims in this tragedy."

TO PAIGE'S SURPRISE, Sergeant Thurlo called later that evening to tell them he'd alerted the city police departments in Toronto, Edmonton and Sudbury and efforts were under way to protect the potential victims and place them under twenty-four-hour surveillance. Kyle Foster in Toronto, a Bay Street executive, remembered a street derelict had taken his picture a couple of weeks ago when he'd gone to a lunch meeting. He'd thought the wino was just playing with a broken camera, but it had given him an eerie feeling.

Foster's financial services company was a major supporter of Olympic-bound Canadian athletes.

When Sergeant Thurlo buzzed the intercom to the condo at noon the next day, Paige hoped there had been a major development. She didn't know whether it was the waiting or the fact that Matt had suggested he sleep in the other guest room last night in deference to her need for space, or the persistent gray drizzle she'd woken up to this morning that had her feeling as if she were climbing the walls. Maybe a combination of all three.

Part of her wished she'd never told him that she might need some time alone, without distractions, to recover her memory. But a restless night listening to water sluice through the gutters and wishing Matt was with her had quickly shown her the error of presuming that having him out of sight would put him out of mind. The truth was, Matt's understanding attitude just made her love him all the more. Drat the man!

Was she being foolish to presume he might want to continue their relationship after all this was over?

You're in no position to be planning a relationship, a voice in her head told her sternly. *You're too vulnerable. You don't even know your own mind.*

An understatement. Paige's lips lifted into a wry smile of welcome as Matt opened the door to Sergeant Thurlo. She supposed she should be used to the sergeant's grim expression, but it hit her like a jab in the stomach. Maybe dealing with robberies, homicides, rapes and all forms of crime on a daily basis left an imprint on a person.

She put down the head of lettuce she was washing in the sink and dried her hands on a towel. "Sergeant. Matt and I were just about to make some lunch. Care to join us?"

"No, thank you."

"Here, I'll take your jacket," Matt offered.

Paige joined them in the pristine living room and perched on the edge of the white damask couch, painfully aware that Matt chose to sit on the love seat. Sergeant Thurlo chose a taupe leather armchair.

"I came by in regard to Joseph Zbarsky," Thurlo began, clearing his throat. "I asked the Ottawa-Carleton Police Department to drop by his house and his cottage when I couldn't reach him by phone at either residence. May I ask when you last spoke to him?"

Paige gulped. Last spoke to him? She glanced at Matt uncertainly. Tendrils of fear snaked around her, cutting off her breathing and her circulation. She felt ice-cold. "Has something happened, Sergeant?"

"I'm sorry to be the one to inform you, but Mr. Zbarsky was found at his Ottawa address a few hours ago. He's been dead for some time. And it wasn't an accident."

"Oh, my God!" The poor man! Paige's throat constricted into a tight knot.

Matt told him the specific day. "We were there in the evening. He told us he was leaving for his cottage the next morning and gave Paige another number to reach him there."

"Was it the same night Paige was nearly struck by a car and went to the hospital?" Thurlo asked.

Paige felt the room spin around her at the implication of the sergeant's question. Had the kidnappers tracked her there and killed Professor Zbarsky because she'd sought out his help? Guilt nipped at her conscience with jagged-edged teeth. She pressed her knees together tightly, trying to maintain control of herself.

"This may or may not be a coincidence, but Zbarsky's black Volvo is missing from his driveway."

"That's the same type of car that tried to run me over last week," she murmured unsteadily.

"Exactly. You said a blue sedan nearly struck you in Ottawa, maybe they decided to change cars. We've got a Canada-wide APB out for it."

Paige managed to hold back the tears until Matt showed Sergeant Thurlo to the door, then she ran to her room and cried.

When Matt knocked on the door several minutes later, she lifted her head from her sodden pillowcase. "Paige? Can I come in?" he asked. The door opened several inches, enough for her to see the compassionate heat of his gaze.

The space between them was far too great.

She stretched out an inviting hand to him. "Oh, Matt! Come and hold me."

Her heart thudded like a leaden bell as his weight dipped onto the mattress and his arms anchored around her, pulling her close. "I'm here as long as you want me, sweetheart."

Paige burrowed her face into his shoulder and hoped he meant every word.

THE HEAT OF THE BATH water and the citrus scent of lemon leaves and orange peels soothed Paige's senses, as did the pleasant song of a robin drifting in through the bathroom window. Paige closed her eyes and admitted to herself that despite the building anxiety over the last ten days of waiting and praying the police would apprehend the kidnappers, she was content in this prison with Matt.

Soulfully content. Which was a bizarre emotion for a woman with amnesia to be experiencing. Maybe she'd just never remember that period of her life because of the head injury she'd sustained. Maybe her feelings for Matt were completely blocking her desire to remember her relationship with Hollis. Or maybe the memories themselves were too painful. Regardless, she was determined to pursue the subject with the psychiatrist when she returned to Montreal. Whenever that would be.

Until then, she was determined to make the most of her time sequestered here with Matt. They'd had a long walk after lunch around the complex until a summer shower had sent them scurrying inside. Paige had told Matt she thought she'd have a nice long bath and take a nap. But thoughts of inviting him to join

her with a bowl of strawberries and a pint of mocha
ice cream drifted deliciously through her mind. Paige
rose and wrapped a towel around her. Then, drying
her feet on the bath mat, she walked down the hall
to give Matt an offer he couldn't refuse. The TV was
on in the living room. At first Paige thought the
voices she heard came from the TV, then she realized
they had a visitor. She probably hadn't heard the bell
with the water running in the tub.

She hung back in the hall and clutched the towel,
listening. Had Sergeant Thurlo returned?

Paige risked taking a peek around the corner into
the living room. Their visitor was Luther Hollis. Why
on earth was he hugging Matt?

Chapter Thirteen

Luther Hollis beamed. "It's over, son. Sergeant Thurlo told me himself. The police arrested three men in Toronto who were attempting to snatch Kyle Foster as he walked to his car in the parking garage after work. They're hoping they'll identify the fourth man soon. Then you can rise from the dead."

"Oh, God, what a relief, Uncle Luther. This has been a nightmare."

"For all of us."

"Did they arrest the man in cowboy boots?"

"I knew you'd ask that. Thurlo said they were all wearing running shoes. But I'm sure it's only a matter of time before they catch that booted bastard, too."

Hollis felt as if a great weight had been partially lifted from his shoulders. He wouldn't feel completely safe though until the fourth man had been arrested. "Let's hope it's soon," he muttered. "This charade has gone on long enough and he could be here in Vancouver right now, hunting Paige."

"Thurlo promised to call when they have more details."

Hollis shot an accusing glance at his uncle. "I

hope he's got an apology ready for Paige. I knew she could be trusted…''

TRUSTED? PAIGE SWAYED as disbelief washed over her in a crushing wave. Matt was Hollis? How could this be? Matt didn't look anything like the picture of Hollis Fenton that Noreen had given her except for— oh, God! Paige closed her eyes, curling her fists in cold fury as she remembered thinking Matt and Hollis both had square jaws. She tried to force her memory to dredge up something that would confirm the awful truth she'd just overheard, but her mind was clogged with confusion.

Matt/Hollis didn't even know the meaning of the word trust. He'd lied to her. Deceived her. Made love to her and had the audacity to put her through some kind of integrity test. If he'd really trusted her, he would have told her who he was long ago—long before they'd made love.

Damn him!

She quietly marched into her room, and eased the door closed. The worst thing about all this, Paige thought miserably, as she dressed, was that she had no idea what Matt's true feelings for her were. Was he just doing and saying whatever he thought necessary to gain her confidence? He certainly hadn't professed undying love for her.

And she wasn't hanging around for any explanations. She threw a change of clothes, the T-shirt she slept in and a few toiletries into her small carry-on suitcase. The kidnappers had been caught and she was going home to celebrate the news with Brenda. She'd stay with Brenda until the fourth man was caught.

Paige cast a last glance around the room. Her clothes weren't fitting all that well anyway; it didn't matter if she abandoned them. Her gaze lingered on the bed where she and Matt had spent so many hours together. His betrayal stung like antiseptic on an open wound. She'd never felt so stupid.

She checked to make sure her wallet was in her purse, then pulled the screen from the open window. With a guilty glance toward the door to her room, she tossed her suitcase out the window onto the lawn beyond the bed of geraniums directly below, and climbed over the sill after it landing in the damp and squishy grass. Then, circling around the condo, she headed for a walking path that would take her to a gate pedestrians used for exiting the complex.

Aware that Matt—she couldn't even think of him as Hollis—might become aware of her departure, or that Luther might leave and notice her walking along the street, Paige quickened her pace. There was a convenience store on Capilano Road—even a motel or two. She'd find a phone and call a taxi to take her to the airport.

It would suit her just fine if she never spoke to Matt Darby, aka Hollis Fenton, ever again.

Twenty minutes later, Paige left the convenience store and veered around the puddles in the parking lot to a pay-phone booth. She had a wallet full of cash thanks to a bank machine in the store, a purse full of snacks and the phone number of a taxi company. The clerk in the convenience store had been kind enough to let her look up the number in the yellow pages directory.

The door to the glass booth didn't shut out the noise of the traffic rushing past in the street. Paige stuck one finger in her ear and tried to understand the dispatcher's questions.

"I want a taxi now. I can't wait twenty minutes," she told him, raising her voice in frustration. "I have a flight to catch." She gave him the street address listed on the phone.

As she hung up the phone, Paige noticed a black car had pulled up alongside the phone booth. A tremor rocked through her when she realized the make of the car was a Mercedes-Benz. Oh, God, had Luther spotted her?

From her angle, she couldn't tell who or how many people were in the car. But to her immense relief the front passenger door opened and a wiry man in a plaid western shirt, slim cut blue jeans and cowboy boots disembarked. Relieved he wasn't Luther or Matt, Paige realized she might be better off waiting for the taxi inside the store.

She bent down and grabbed the strap of the carry-on bag, slipping it over her shoulder. When she straightened, the man was waiting outside the booth with an impatient smile.

"I'm finished," she told him as she pushed the door open.

"You bet you are, missy." The man's expression quickly turned menacing. To her shock, he blocked her way and pressed a gun into her ribs. "Don't scream or your baby won't live long enough to be born. Now get in the car. There's someone who'd like to talk to you."

Fear gripped Paige's heart as he opened the door and shoved her into the back seat.

HOLLIS WAITED UNTIL after his uncle had departed to wake Paige and tell her the news of the kidnappers' arrest. When she didn't respond to his light knock, he opened the door a crack and peeked inside. "Paige? Wake up, sweetheart. I've got some great news."

At first glance he realized Paige wasn't in the room and the bed hadn't been slept on. His gaze swept the room looking at details. There was no sign of her purse and the tube of hand cream she used before she went to sleep was no longer on the night stand. He yanked the closet door open and swore.

Her small suitcase was missing. Then he noticed the open window.

Hollis groaned in dismay when he looked out the window and saw the trampled flower bed. What the hell did Paige think she was doing?

For a second Hollis couldn't breathe as doubts poisoned the air in his lungs. Why would Paige leave? Had she suddenly recovered her memory? Or had she overheard his conversation with his uncle?

A third possibility kicked him solidly in the gut. Was it possible the fourth kidnapper—Cowboy Boots—had finally located her and had dragged her away against her will?

Hollis scrambled over the windowsill and sat back on his heels in the damp grass to examine the footprints in the soft, moist earth. There were only one kind and they didn't resemble in the least the shape that could be left by a boot.

Which meant, that for whatever reason, Paige had left under her own steam. Had she finally figured out who he was? He dug into his front pocket and removed the key ring that held the keys to the condo, the complex and the car in the garage. The car key was still there leaving Hollis to conclude she had to have left on foot.

Pushing back his fears Hollis sprinted toward the garage. If she was on foot, she couldn't have gotten far.

"AH, MISS ROBERTS, so we meet again. I knew Luther would lead us to you sooner or later."

Paige couldn't see who was speaking to her from behind the wheel of the car—not with her abductor's hands forcing her cheek down onto the leather seat. The headrest concealed the back of the man's head, but she could see enough of a shoulder to tell he was wearing a dark suit. And something about the man's voice and the heavy musky scent in the car seemed vaguely familiar.

With a start, Paige wondered if she'd been in this car before. Then she saw the head of the cane wedged between the front seats. The face of a wolf glowered at her with gleaming jet eyes and teeth bared.

Her head started to pound and nausea lifted and rolled in her stomach. Her mouth went bone dry and her vision blurred. Suddenly an image filled her mind—of a man in a trench coat, a hat pulled low over his face and a cell phone pressed to his ear, murmuring an apology the day of the explosion. She'd been so distracted by the thought of her reunion with Hollis as she'd hurried down the sidewalk, that she'd barely noticed the little old man standing near a streetlight, much less his cane, until she'd tripped over it.

Paige moaned when she remembered Hollis as she'd seen him that day, whole and handsome, his hair glinting in the sun as he crossed the parking lot.

Then the vision exploded into a thousand shards. "Oh, my God. It was you!" she exclaimed, trying to push herself up.

The man beside her thumped her in the face with the flat of his hand. "Stay down."

Pain numbed her cheek and jaw. Paige screamed and tried to kick him only to feel the nose of the gun dig sharply into her waist.

"Don't hurt her," Ken Whitfield ordered calmly from the front seat. "She's an expectant mother. I just want to come to an understanding with her."

Cold perspiration beaded on Paige's skin. "An understanding? How could you ever expect me to understand why you would kill your own son-in-law?"

"So you know that much, do you?"

"Yes," Paige admitted hoarsely. She tried to fight back the bile rising in her throat. Oh, God, she was going to be car sick! "The police suspect Hollis's kidnapping was a copycat crime, too. And they'll confirm it when they interrogate the men they arrested today in Toronto. You might have gotten away with it if you'd killed Hollis when you left him on Mount Seymour instead of releasing him so he could tell the police that he had four abductors. The other victims were abducted by three men. And you screwed up big time with the hood."

"Oh, I'm not particularly worried about the men they arrested today sharing too much information with the police. And let me assure you that I particularly enjoyed the symbolism in restraining Hollis and releasing him, only to have his life literally blow up in his face. That's what he did to Christine. And he deserved to be punished."

"Why?" Paige demanded, struggling to make sense out of Whitfield's twisted reasoning.

"Because he killed her. She loved him. She wanted to make him happy and have babies. But he wouldn't let her. She took the baby from the hospital because she was convinced that showing him she could take care of a baby would make him love her more. And that bastard contacted the police. A judge ordered her committed to a mental hospital to determine whether she was mentally fit to stand trial. It took some doing, but I helped her escape. We were going to go to the Caribbean together—far away from Hollis Fenton. We got stopped in traffic on the bridge leading to the airport. Before I knew what was happening, Christine opened the door to the car and jumped off the bridge." Whitfield's voice broke. "She didn't want to live without that bastard. He'd told her he was going to divorce her because she was sick. I wanted Hollis to know what it was like to be held against his will, only to be given his freedom and then have his life cruelly end."

Paige gagged and choked back tears, wishing she could remember what Hollis might have shared with her about Christine before the explosion. She didn't trust anything "Matt" or Noreen had told her. "I'm sorry you lost your daughter in such a terribly tragic way. But do you think Christine would have wanted you to hurt the one person she loved so much?"

"Christine is gone. People who haven't experienced loss have no idea how final death is. Memories don't comfort you, they only make you more bitter. I lived for Christine. She was the center of my world and now I have nothing."

Paige closed her eyes at the pain resonating in Ken

Whitfield's voice. His words hit so close to home. Ever since she'd found out she was pregnant, the baby growing in her had become the center of her world. And she was terrified that she'd never get to hold her child in her arms. Ken Whitfield sounded emotionally unstable.

Courage, a voice whispered in her mind. "W-where are you taking me?" she asked.

"Someplace quiet where we can talk undisturbed."

Her stomach rolled again as the car went around a curve. Paige tried to breathe in and out slowly. "Why don't you pull over now?" she suggested. "I'm getting car sick and I think I'm going to throw up."

"And give you a chance to scream or escape? I think not. Surely you must understand, Ms. Roberts, how Christine would have felt knowing another woman carried her husband's child? Evelyn thought I would find the news comforting in my grief over Hollis's death."

Oh, God, Paige thought, with mounting panic. He was going to kill her. And he would kill Hollis, too, once he learned he'd survived the explosion.

HOLLIS PULLED INTO the parking lot of the convenience store with a squealing of tires and left the keys hanging in the ignition as he leapt from the car. An electronic bell pinged and a pimply faced clerk with bleached stripes in his hair tensed at the counter when he burst into the store.

"I'm looking for my wife," Hollis said breathlessly. "We had an argument and she packed a bag. I think she may have walked here to get some cash. Have you seen her?"

''Is she cute and blond?'' the clerk asked.

''Yes, and pregnant.''

''Well, that explains the candy bars and the yogurt. You just missed her. She called a taxi but—''

Hollis swore, cutting him off and jabbed his fingers through his miserably short hair. ''Did she say where she might be going?''

''Well, she mentioned she needed the snacks 'cause she hated airplane food...''

Hollis opened his wallet and thrust a twenty at the clerk. ''Thanks you've been really helpful. I'll try to catch her at the airport.''

''But mister—''

The bell sounded again as someone entered the store. Hollis whirled around, hoping to see Paige. A man with bushy white eyebrows and heavy jowls stood frowning in the doorway. ''Did someone here call for a taxi?''

''Sorry, man,'' the clerk called out. ''It's just like I was trying to tell her husband here, she got another ride.''

Hollis turned back to the clerk. ''You could have told me someone gave her a ride.''

The clerk rubbed the side of his cheek. ''I tried, but you didn't give me a chance.''

Hollis laid another twenty on the counter. ''Now's your chance.''

''She was on the phone and a guy came up to her at the phone booth and started talking to her. Next thing I know she's getting into a black car with him.''

''What type of car?''

''I don't know. I wasn't paying that much attention. I had other customers, but I had the impression it was expensive—probably a Mercedes-Benz or a BMW.''

''Which way did they go?''

''They headed north up the road.''

North? That was the direction of the condo. If Paige were leaving him, she'd have headed south down to Marine Drive which was a main arterial route. ''Are you sure they headed north?''

''I'm positive.''

Hollis's thoughts raced. His uncle drove a black Jaguar. Maybe he'd noticed Paige and offered her a lift. But then again, the car that had nearly struck Paige a week ago Saturday had been a black Volvo. Was it possible Cowboy Boots had followed Luther to the condo?

Hollis held firm to the hope that Paige and Luther would be at the condo when he got there, because the other possibility left him sweating with fear. He was hardly aware of his actions or the traffic as he sped up to the intersection and made a left turn onto the road that led back to the complex.

But to his dismay, there was no sign of his uncle's sports car in the visitor's parking space in front of the condo. And the condo was excruciatingly silent. But the clerk had seemed certain the black car had headed north. Capilano Road wove up the mountain to a regional park with tourist attractions, though there were on and off ramps to connect with the Upper Levels Highway. Had Luther taken Paige to his home in the British Properties?

Sweat trickled between Hollis's shoulder blades as he punched in his uncle's cell phone number. Luther answered immediately.

"Uncle Luther? Paige is gone. Please tell me you have her and you're taking her to your house."

"No, son. I haven't seen her. I just walked back into the office. What do you mean she's gone?"

Hollis hastily explained.

"Do you think she's been kidnapped?" Luther demanded.

"Possibly." Anxiety shredded Hollis's stomach into a thousand strings. He was achingly aware of all the isolated wooded spots in the Capilano Canyon Regional Park where someone could dump a body. "I'm calling the police."

"I'm coming right over, son."

"Good. I'm going to try driving up the road. Maybe I'll see something."

Hollis hurried back to his car and used his cellular phone to call Sergeant Thurlo. His impulse was to burn rubber as he drove up Capilano Road, but he forced himself to slow down so he'd have a better chance of spotting Paige.

"Mr. Fenton," Sergeant Thurlo said, finally coming on the line. "I suppose you're pleased with the news."

"I'll be more pleased when you tell me you've caught the fourth man. Paige is missing. A clerk in a convenience store saw her get into a black car with a man that headed north up Capilano Road. The clerk thought the car was a Mercedes or a BMW. I'm driving up Capilano now, but I don't see any sign of her yet. I have a bad feeling they're headed toward the park."

"I wish I could tell you the fourth man was in custody, but I can't. We've identified the other three and we're interviewing everyone we can to see if we can find the fourth operative. But I can tell you that they're all in their late forties to early fifties, brilliant men in management positions who were pushed out of jobs by corporate downsizing two Christmases ago. We believe the kidnappings were their way of funding their retirement.''

Hollis swore. "Have they admitted to anything?"

"Nope. They're not talking. But we don't like the idea that the fourth operative is out on the loose."

Hollis slammed on the brakes to avoid running a red light as Thurlo's words came back to him. He couldn't describe even one of his abductors as being capable of brilliance. And the appointment article in *The Globe and Mail* had appeared in November *before* those men lost their jobs. "Tell me something. Did the kidnappers have a hood on them?"

"Yes."

"What type of fabric was it made out of?"

"Cotton—like the others."

"Mine was made of velvet," Hollis said curtly. He wondered if his uncle had really returned to his office or if he was, even now, dragging Paige out into the woods to her death. Was his uncle trying to ensure that he never took over as CEO of the Hollis Group—or protecting the actions of one of his sons? Hollis couldn't imagine his cousin Sandford using his own cell phone to set off the bomb. But one of Luther's sons might have thought it damnably funny to implicate Sandford in his murder. Hollis felt physically ill.

"You might think I'm off the wall, Sergeant, but I have a pretty sick feeling that someone in my family orchestrated a copycat kidnapping and might have Paige now. My uncle drives a black sports car and he was at the condo to supposedly tell me the three kidnappers were caught before she disappeared. Paige would trust him enough to get in a car with him.''

Thurlo exhaled sharply. "Let's not take any chances. I'll contact the North Vancouver RCMP and have them dispatch some cars to the area. There are three parking lots up there that I'm aware of. One at the fish hatchery, one at the dam and one at the Grouse Mountain ski resort.''

''I'll try the fish hatchery first.''

Before Thurlo could protest, Hollis hung up. Then he called his cousin Sandford's office.

Sandford's secretary expressed shock at hearing his voice. Sandford's surprise was more evident.

"Are you crazy? Maria recognized your voice. Mom called a few minutes ago to tell me the kidnappers had been arrested, but don't you think it would be prudent to wait a few days before you announce you're still alive? What if the police made a mistake?''

''That's why I'm calling, Sand. I want to make sure the police didn't make a mistake. I understand your cellular phone was stolen while you were at a Vancouver Board of Trade conference. Was anyone in the family at the same conference?''

''Why do you ask?''

''Just answer the question! It's important.''

''I hope you're not suggesting I had anything to do with this.'' Sand sounded truly offended.

Hollis pulled into the entrance to the fish hatchery. The parking lot held at least a dozen cars. None of them black. Gritting his teeth, he whipped the car around in a rapid U-turn, leaving a trail of rubber on the pavement.

"No, I don't think you had anything to do with it. I think you were set up. Come on, Sand, think. Who else was there?" Hollis turned back onto Capilano Road.

"No one, I swear. Unless you count Christine's dad."

"Ken was there?"

"Yes. He was the keynote speaker."

Hollis dropped the phone and clung to the steering wheel with both hands as he made a sharp turn onto the entrance lane to the parking lot of the Cleveland Dam. Suddenly, all the pieces fit together.

"THE COUPLE IS GONE. Get her out of the car. Quickly. We don't want any tourists showing up and capturing this special moment on film," Ken Whitfield directed his hired thug.

"Sure, boss."

Paige drew in a gulp of air that didn't smell like dirt and grimy sweat as the hand which had been clamped over her mouth for what felt like eons was finally removed. Her legs were numb and dipped beneath her as she was jerked out of the backseat of the car.

The thug Whitfield had called Shane snaked an iron-hard arm around her waist and gripped her arm in a vicious hold just above her elbow. Paige screamed and tried to twist away from him. She didn't have any idea where they were. Beyond the parking lot all she could see was a large grassy area bordering a lake. A chain-link fence prevented people from getting too close to the water's edge. Tall, dark evergreens ringed the area. Maybe if she could get free she could hide in the trees.

"Scream all you want, no one will hear you," Shane said, with a grin, poking the gun into her ribs.

Paige kicked him in the leg with her sandaled foot. A definite mistake. He was wearing cowboy boots. Pain streaked through her toes. Shane dragged her toward what looked like a bridge spanning this end of the lake, while Ken Whitfield followed more slowly, limping with his cane. Paige noticed he carried her bag and her purse.

She knew they were going to shoot her. What difference did it make if they shot her now or later? Except that someone might notice blood in the parking lot and report it to the police and her body might be found.

Paige fought like a wildcat, trying to rake her nails down Shane's face. Her head pounded and the nausea welled in her throat as she kicked and clawed, expecting any second to hear the gun go off and put an end to her misery.

Shane only laughed and squeezed her arm tighter as if he enjoyed her terror.

They'd reached the bridge.

"Pull her out to the center, Shane," Whitfield directed. "We can't throw her over the fence here. The drop isn't steep enough. There's only a rail in the center. Give me the gun, you'll need both hands."

To her horror, Paige realized they weren't on a bridge, but on the top of a dam. Now she could hear the sound of the water. The sheer vertical drop into the mist formed by the water thundering through the gates into the Capilano River below would kill her.

They didn't intend to shoot her. Whitfield wanted

her to suffer the same fate as his daughter. People would think she'd killed herself over Hollis's death after the details of their relationship were revealed.

Courage, the voice urged her again, resonating in her brain through the pounding of her head, strengthening her for a final fight.

"No!" she screamed, clasping her arms around Shane's neck as he tried to lift her and throw her over the rail.

A shout reached her ears over the roar of the water; a voice Paige recognized that tore at her heart. She wasn't alone. Paige reacted instinctively. She threw up on Shane and prayed Whitfield didn't know how to use that gun.

Chapter Fourteen

Hollis's heart lodged in his throat when he saw the lone black Mercedes-Benz in the parking lot. His pulse raced faster than the engine of his car as he scanned the thick growth of trees skirting the parking area for some sign of Paige or a path that offered immediate seclusion from prying eyes.

Where the hell were they?

His gaze shifted across the grassy playing area to the dam. And then he saw the three figures moving on top of the dam and recognized Paige's golden hair.

Oh, God. Paige.

Her flailing arms meant she was still alive, and relief surged through him as he pressed the gas pedal to the floor. Upright metal posts set into the concrete barred his ability to drive up on the dam itself. He got as close as he could, then put the car in park and flew out the door.

He couldn't even feel his feet touching the ground. All he saw was the gun in Ken's hands and a man wearing cowboy boots struggling with Paige, lifting her up and carrying her toward the railing. Ken threw Paige's purse and her small suitcase over the rail.

"Ken, no!" he shouted at the top of his lungs. Bands of fear tightened around him as he realized they meant to throw Paige off the dam next.

Ken whirled around at the sound of his name, his eyes widening.

"No, you bastard! You couldn't stop Christine, but you can stop this."

"Hollis?" Ken looked as if he'd seen a ghost. But the next moment, his ex-father-in-law raised his arm and fired.

Hollis didn't know by what miracle Ken's shot missed him, but he didn't stop to question it. Paige bless her, was throwing up on her captor, who released her with an exclamation of disgust. Hollis launched himself at the man in cowboy boots, taking him down hard on the concrete walkway. They rolled and Hollis lit into the man, who'd so brutally tortured him, as if he were a punching bag.

Paige took advantage of her second of freedom to grab Ken's cane. Wielding it like a baseball bat, she struck the hand which held the gun.

Ken cried out in pain as the gun landed about eight feet away and skittered farther along the walkway. Ken moved toward it, but Paige pushed him out of the way and reached it first. She was about to pick it up to throw it over the railing when she heard the sirens and saw two police cars pull into the parking lot behind them, lights flashing. She put her foot down on top of the gun as Hollis clamped a hand on Ken's shoulder and whirled him around.

"You can't kill me, you bastard," he breathed, slamming his fist into Ken's jaw. "I'm already dead."

Ken slumped to the ground.

Hollis reached for Paige, but a police officer called out for him to freeze and put his hands in the air. He had the feeling the police officer's aim was a lot surer than Ken's.

"Is one of you Matt Darby?" the same officer asked as they were surrounded by four police officers with guns drawn.

"I am," Hollis said. "She's Paige Roberts."

"Step away from the weapon, ma'am."

"Are you okay?" Hollis asked Paige as a female officer bent down and retrieved the gun.

"I'm fine, Hollis. I couldn't be better."

"This gun's been fired," the female officer commented.

"Ken Whitfield fired it at Hollis when he tried to stop the other man—Shane—I don't know his last name—from throwing me off the dam," Paige explained, out of breath. "He wanted me to die the same way his daughter died."

The first officer frowned. "Why do you keep calling him Hollis?" he demanded. "I thought you said your name was Matt? Okay, folks, let's see some ID."

"I don't have any ID. Whitfield threw my purse over the dam."

Every nerve in Hollis's body twittered with alarm and it had nothing to do with being surrounded by four cops who wanted to know what the hell was going on. He passed one of the cops his wallet, relieved that two other officers were cuffing Ken and the man in the cowboy boots and leading them away. But he had eyes only for Paige. "You called me Hollis," he said to her. "Does that mean—"

Her silver eyes glittered, overflowing with distrust.

"It means I know you for the liar that you are. Of-ficer," she pleaded with a determined lift of her chin to the female cop, "please get me as far away from this man as possible."

"Paige—"

"Leave me the hell alone."

Hollis tried to follow her, but the first officer put a restraining hand on his arm. Judging by the rigid line of Paige's shoulders as she walked away from him, Hollis suspected the price he would pay for test-ing her honesty would be the loss of her love.

HOLLIS STARED OUT at the panorama of mountains outside his office window, his thoughts thousands of miles away in Montreal. It had been five days since Ken had been arrested. Every bone in his body urged him to leap on a plane and fly east to explain his side of things to Paige. Paige's father had phoned Luther to assure him she'd arrived home safely and was staying with them, but apart from that, Hollis had heard nothing directly from Paige.

He was worried he never would.

How much more space should he give her? They had a baby on the way they needed to talk about and he wasn't going to be excluded from his child's life. He didn't want to be excluded from Paige's life ei-ther.

Sergeant Thurlo had explained to him Paige's ver-sion of events. She'd left the condo after overhearing his Uncle Luther tell him the kidnappers had been arrested. Seeing Ken's cane when she was forced into his car had triggered her to recall bumping into Ken the morning of the explosion, but that was all.

Hollis sighed.

Ken had confessed to orchestrating his kidnapping and now he seemed hell-bent on letting the world know why he thought Hollis had deserved to be punished for Christine's death. Hollis found it difficult to feel anything but pity for Ken, though he was relieved Shane Morrison had ratted on the other three men Ken had hired to do his dirty work and all four were safely behind bars awaiting trial.

Ken had been a wonderful father to Christine. Who could blame a man who loved his child and tried so hard to protect her? Hollis couldn't generate enough emotional energy to do so. Ken had made mistakes, but Hollis admitted he had, too. He deeply regretted telling Christine he'd divorce her if she didn't agree to take her medication. But she'd abducted a baby and put its parents through an unspeakable trauma that Ken thought they could all sweep under the rug with a hefty settlement. Hollis had been wild with worry over what could happen next. In retrospect, if they'd all been more honest with each other, maybe Christine wouldn't have taken her life.

Hollis had made the same mistake with Paige and he realized it. He just didn't know whether or not this mistake was irreparable.

A knock sounded briskly on the door and Hollis turned quickly in his chair, half hoping to see Paige.

But it was Noreen. She held an envelope in her hands and her face was pale. ''This just arrived for you by courier from Montreal. It's from a lawyer's office.''

Hollis read the label on the cardboard envelope she placed on his desk: Maidment, Roth & Savard, Barristers and Solicitors. Why did he have the feeling his future was mapped out in whatever was in that envelope?

"Thanks, Noreen."

He waited until Noreen had closed the door softly behind her before he opened the envelope. It contained a letter from Paige's lawyer stating her terms.

Hollis read the two-page letter twice and felt as if his heart had been stuffed with cotton wool. The letter informed him Paige was seeking therapy with a psychiatrist. For her own health and the health of the baby, she preferred not to discuss their relationship until she recovered her memory. Until then, if he wished her to respect his rights to access to their child, he was not to contact her in any way. She'd notify him of the baby's birth and they'd work out some kind of visitation agreement through their lawyers.

She had him boxed into a corner.

SIX MONTHS LATER the ringing of the phone jarred Hollis from a restless night's sleep. "Hollis Fenton?" a woman with a French accent said. "I'm Brenda Thompson."

Hollis sat straight up in bed. "I know who you are. You're Paige's friend."

Brenda laughed. In the background Hollis could hear a loudspeaker. "I may not be much longer if she finds out I've called you. Paige is in labor—"

"But she's not due for another two and a half weeks," Hollis spluttered.

"The first thing you learn about babies is that they come whenever they're ready."

"I'll be on the first plane I can get."

"I hoped you'd say that. Seeing our baby being

born was the happiest moment in Claude's life.''
Brenda gave him the name of the hospital and the
floor number and Hollis hung up in a daze. He was
going to be a father.

That took some of the sting out of the knowledge
that Paige didn't want him with her. Every day he'd
waited expectantly for the phone to ring and spent
his evenings writing letters addressed to their baby.
He had a special box for the letters and he planned
to give them to his new son or daughter. He didn't
want his child ever doubting his love.

Hollis jumped out of bed and started packing,
blessing Brenda Thompson for her compassion.
Brenda was right. He had just as much right to be in
the delivery room as Paige did. He just hoped he
wouldn't be too late.

"OKAY, PAIGE, YOU'VE come this far. You're fully
dilated. It's time to push with the next contraction.''

Paige sagged against the birthing chair contraption,
completely exhausted. She'd been in labor over
twenty-four hours, with the baby pressing up against
her back. She'd walked, done breathing exercises and
discovered to her dismay as the labor pains increased
in strength, that after years of turning her nose up at
most drugs, she just wanted to be put out of her misery. She'd practically begged for an epidural. And
now the darn thing was wearing off. Why, oh, why
didn't this baby want to come out?

She'd be a good mother. She promised.

Brenda rubbed her shoulder. ''Come on, this is the
part where mothers earn their Victoria Crosses. It
separates the women from the weenies.''

"We've got another contraction starting. Push, Paige," her doctor instructed.

Paige closed her eyes and pushed with all her might until she thought her head would explode from the pressure, not to mention other parts of her.

"Take a rest and wait for the next one," her doctor said. "I can see the head."

The head. *Please, baby. Please come,* Paige thought wearily.

The doors to the delivery room suddenly swung open and a man strode in as if he had all the authority in the world. He was dressed in sterile hospital garb like everyone else in the room. Paige wondered if he was the chief ob gyn and had come to find out what was taking so long with this particular delivery. God, what if someone had sent for him because the baby was in distress?

Then his gaze met hers and Paige forgot to breathe. A shock of blond hair peeped below the pale blue cap covering his head. Hazel eyes flecked with gold dared her to demand that she leave. She recognized those eyes.

Hollis.

"I'm the father," he said curtly and walked right up to her, taking the side of the birthing bed opposite Brenda.

Paige couldn't come up with an argument as another contraction welled through her with the unstoppable force of a tidal wave.

Paige focused within herself and pushed, deeply aware that she'd gripped Hollis's hand and was holding on for dear life.

Minutes later, their baby entered the world.

"It's a boy," her doctor cried out.

A boy! Tears welled in Paige's eyes as Hollis helped her lean forward to see the tiny infant a nurse was swaddling in a towel. Oh, God, he was beautiful!

He opened scrunched up eyes and peered at the lights as if wondering what the fuss was all about. Paige was so tired she didn't have the strength to resist the joy that overcame her when the nurse put their baby in Hollis's arms first. Hollis beamed proudly and Paige felt the tears slip onto her cheeks when he said hello to his son and told him he loved him. Then, he carefully set their baby in Paige's arms.

She had never held anything so precious.

"We did something very very right," he murmured close to her ear. "I hope you remember that always."

Paige couldn't put off telling him the truth any longer. "I do remember, Hollis," she said softly. "I got my memory back about six weeks ago. I didn't contact you because my blood pressure was rising due to my pregnancy and I didn't want to upset myself and place the baby at risk."

She gazed up at him steadily. He was waiting for her to continue, but the longer she looked into the warmth centering in those familiar hazel eyes, the more uncertain she became of her feelings. With the proof of their attraction to each other nestled cozily in her arms, she could readily admit that the man standing before her resembled the Hollis Fenton she'd met in Vancouver, who'd captured her heart and her interest, but her feelings were so intertwined with his betrayal she couldn't trust them.

And she had no idea what his true feelings had been for her. She'd met his family. Distrust ran so rampant among them they were afraid to turn their backs on each other. For all she knew, the only reason Hollis was here was because he didn't trust her to care for the baby on her own. Her arms tightened protectively around their son. "And frankly," she continued, "I didn't see what there was to talk about that our lawyers couldn't handle. Your actions spoke for themselves."

Hollis felt as if a part of him were being snuffed out. The cold determination in Paige's tone hinted there was very little room for negotiation. But he wasn't letting go of their relationship this easily, not when they could have so much more together. "I understand why you're hurt," he said quietly, "but I'd still—"

"Excuse me," a nurse cut in, reaching for the baby. "This little one needs to be weighed and measured. And our poor tired mom needs her rest. So everybody out."

Hollis felt a light touch on his arm. "That means us, Mr. Fenton," a woman with dark eyes told him. "I'm Brenda Thompson." To his surprise, she kissed him on both cheeks. "Thank you for everything you've done to find the men who killed my husband. And for saving Paige. She's a good friend. I don't know what I'd do without her."

Hollis didn't know how he would cope without her either. He looked back at Paige, reluctant to leave with so much unsettled between them, but she was already turning her face away from him.

Damn. Was it really over?

"Do I even have a chance?" Hollis asked Brenda when he bought her a cup of coffee in the hospital cafeteria after he'd taken a roll of pictures of the baby as he was tended to in the nursery. Brenda had introduced him to Paige's parents and her sister. His reception had been tepid to say the least. No less than he deserved. Hollis had told her father straight out that he loved Paige and he wanted to marry her. Paige's father had wryly wished him luck.

Brenda added a packet of sweetener to her coffee. "I honestly don't know if you have a chance of working things out with Paige." Minus her hospital disguise, Hollis could see Brenda was a slender woman with a dark mane of curly hair and a smile that transformed her ordinary features into an expression of natural beauty. "I do know that being a single parent is not the same experience as raising a child in a loving, committed relationship."

Hollis squeezed her hand, knowing she was thinking of Claude.

"I think she loves you, but she isn't sure who you really are and which feelings she can trust," Brenda continued.

"Well then, I'll just give her my heart and trust her to know what to do with it."

PAIGE SLEPT FOR SIX HOURS. When she awoke it was three o'clock in the morning and her breasts felt as if they'd hardened into stone. Her milk was coming in. She climbed out of bed and walked stiffly to the bathroom, noticing that while she'd been asleep someone had deposited a large gift bag with a brightly colored "It's A Boy" balloon attached on the comfortable chair in the room. Probably Brenda. Paige was about to find her way to the nursery for a bonding session with her son when a nurse entered her room, wheeling a bassinet.

A plaintive wail, like a mewling kitten, told Paige she'd been missed.

"Oh, good, you're awake," the nurse said. "We've got a very hungry young man here. Climb back into bed. We'll get the two of you settled."

Paige sighed with trepidation and wonder as her son started to suckle at her breast a few minutes later.

The nurse gave her an encouraging smile. "You're making good progress. If you're hungry, you'll find snacks and sandwiches in the mother's lounge next door to the nursery. By the way, the special delivery there is from the baby's father. He asked me to tell you it was a gift for the baby. He said he'd wait to hear from you."

So Hollis had respected her wishes and left town already. Paige supposed she should feel relieved.

"Thank you."

The nurse told her everything she needed to change the baby was on the bassinet cart and to buzz if she needed help.

Paige stroked the soft golden down covering her son's head and decided her first parenting decision would be to come up with a name. Though daunted by the prospect of being responsible for his health and well-being, she suspected this handsome young man would be just as adept at commandeering her attention and her emotions as he had while he was in her womb. He was going to be quite the little distraction.

Just like his father.

Though she hadn't been a good candidate for hypnotism, Paige's memory had returned in bits and pieces. Now she remembered all too clearly the whirlwind feelings of being swept off her feet by an intelligent, sexy man, who made her laugh, and spending an incredible night in his bed. She'd awakened early the next morning, nearly bursting with the desire to share her feelings for him, but she'd held back and gone to do an interview in White Rock, thinking it was too soon to tell the difference between infatuation and love when they'd only known each other a week.

She'd agreed to meet him at his condo for dinner, but he wasn't there when she arrived. She'd thought she had misunderstood their meeting place and called her hotel to see if there were any messages. She'd known something was horribly wrong when she was given an urgent message to call Noreen. Paige thought her heart would stop when Noreen told her Luther had received a call notifying him that Hollis had been abducted.

Paige didn't want to remember those anxious three days when she couldn't sleep or eat and was afraid to move more than an arm length's distance from the phone. She just wanted Hollis to be safe.

Blessedly, she could only recall snatches of the morning of the explosion. She was too distracted by her first glimpse of Hollis as he climbed out of his car to pay much attention to Ken Whitfield when she tripped over his cane. She was too busy reassuring herself that Hollis was in one piece. She'd called out his name and her heart had lifted when he broke into a broad grin and cut across the parking lot toward her.

Some nights Paige allowed herself the luxury of wondering what might have happened between them if the bomb hadn't exploded. Other nights she ridiculed herself for not being more suspicious of Matt.

But most of the time it just hurt knowing that Hollis had lied to her and betrayed her trust because he suspected she might be involved in his kidnapping.

She glanced over at the gift bag. Even when Hollis was out of her life he succeeded in distracting her.

She finished feeding the baby, smiling at her success in getting a burp out of him, changed his very wet diaper and carried him over to the chair with her, snuggling his warm little body in her lap.

''Let's see what your daddy has brought you.''

There were four wrapped packages inside the bag. And they were numbered. Curious, Paige opened the package marked number one first. She exclaimed out loud when she saw the hand-painted box decorated with figures from nursery rhymes. She ran her fingers over the cow jumping over the moon and a dish running away with a spoon. The detailing was exquisite. The box looked old enough to be an antique.

When she lifted the lid she found a stack of letters addressed, ''To My Baby'' in a strong, bold hand.

Paige unfolded the first letter. The pale blue pages trembled when she saw the first line. She read it aloud:

I never really knew my father. His name was Matthew Fenton. He left when I was three years old. I don't remember much about him—except that he was an artist and sometimes would read to me from a book called, *The Velveteen Rabbit*. He made this box for me when I was born. I used to play with it when I was younger and wonder why he wasn't living with my mother and me. I told myself he was too busy illustrating picture books and castles to be with us. But

deep down I always thought it was because he
didn't love us.

I'm not certain what the future holds for your
mother and me. Maybe we won't live together
as a family. But I don't want you to ever doubt
that I love you or that I don't want to be your
father. This box is my promise to you to be more
than a stranger in your life.

The baby made a little mewl of approval. Paige
reluctantly reached for the next letter in the box. Hollis's account of his childhood exploits made her
laugh until she came to a long passage about his family and his cousins and how he'd felt he never truly
belonged in their midst. He'd realized only recently
that he'd never given them enough credit. He'd expected them to abandon him like his father had, but
when he'd really needed them most, they'd rallied
behind him.

Paige assumed Hollis was referring to his kidnapping ordeal. The next few letters were about his
mother and her twin sister Evelyn and the years Hollis spent at university getting a degree in business.
Paige cried when she learned his mother died of
breast cancer just before he graduated.

There were more letters. About his rise up the corporate ladder of the family company. About his Uncle Luther. Even a letter about his first marriage to
Christine and his hurt and confusion that she was sick
and didn't tell him. Paige tried to numb her heart to
the emotions in the letters and the stories that filled
in the chinks between the facts of Hollis's life like
mortar. He'd given his son the story of his life in a
box and though his words showed his clever wit and

an ability to laugh at himself, Paige saw all too clearly a distrustful little boy who'd grown into a man, who was still afraid he'd be abandoned by the people who were supposed to love him.

There was only one letter left. Paige was almost afraid to open it. Hollis's words leapt off the page and pierced her heart:

The first time I saw your mother I knew she was special and rare. She made me think of the antique glass Christmas decorations my mother used to collect—delicate and beautiful, glistening silver and gold. After my wife died, I wasn't sure whether I wanted to care about anyone ever again. But when your mother sashayed into my office and smiled at me, her eyes shining with candor and integrity and determination to help her friend, she captured my soul. And when she spoke to me, she completely captured my fancy.

Even though I'd already eaten, I invited her out to lunch because I didn't want her to leave. By the time we finished lunch I was trying to figure out how I was going to convince this journalist from Montreal that she was my destiny.

Paige felt her breath grow still in her lungs as she rapidly skimmed the rest of the letter. Conflicting emotions warred in her when Hollis explained that he trusted her so much he refused to believe Sergeant Thurlo's theory that Paige may have somehow been involved in the kidnappings and might be feigning amnesia. He even withheld from the police information that Noreen had found in Paige's belongings which might implicate Paige in his kidnapping. He wasn't going to go into hiding and leave her to the mercy of the police. Not when the image of her beautiful, smiling face had given him the courage to survive the ordeal. His confession that he planned to tell her he loved her and wanted to marry her the morning they were to meet at his office brought a thick lump of tears to her throat.

Yes, Hollis admitted, he could have told her who he was, but he wanted Paige to remember who he was and if he was special to her on her own. He respected her wishes to stay away because she's still the same refreshingly honest woman he fell in love with and he will always take her at her word and trust her to do what's best for their child.

It wasn't quite an apology for having the arrogance to waltz into her life and her heart as another man, but it was an explanation. Paige folded the letter and wiped the tears off her cheeks, ever conscious of the baby's warmth burrowed against her. The baby dozed like an angel, calmly entrusting her to judiciously determine his future. Her heart ached with indecision as she withdrew the package marked number two from the bag.

It was a much worn, and much read copy of *The Velveteen Rabbit*. Hollis's book saved from his childhood? Paige clutched it to her chest and sobbed. Part of her was terribly angry that he'd betrayed her. But another part was angrier still at the idea of a little boy yearning for his father's love.

It was a long while before she had the courage to open the package marked number three. The enormous, plush teddy bear with a wistful expression brought a smile to her face. As did the name tag attached to the red satin ribbon tied around the caramel bear's neck. The bear's name was ''Daddy Bear.'' Hollis had written on the tag, ''For Bear Hugs when Daddy is far away.''

Paige thought it was very easy to love a sensitive man. She just didn't know whether or not she was capable of forgiving him. She wouldn't let Hollis's explanations or his gifts weaken her resolve to give her baby a happy home based on trust.

With a small sigh, she tore the brightly-colored paper off a brick-sized gift marked number four. This package weighed little more than a feather. Inside a nest of tissue paper Paige found a glass Christmas ornament. It was six inches long. The top was a round gold sphere etched with snowflakes that tapered off in a silver shaft to a small gold sphere at the bottom, where a tiny snowflake was etched.

It glistened in the semi-darkened room, winking with the promise and the magic of Christmas.

Paige was packing the letter and the gifts back into the bag when there was a light tap at the door. She swung around expecting to see a nurse coming to bring the baby back to the nursery, but it was Hollis.

HE LOOKED EVEN more handsome and more familiar than he had in hospital garb last night. The golden shock of hair drifted onto his forehead above eyes that gleamed at her in amusement. Something about his eyebrows looked different, too. They were fuller and blonder. But she could still see the scar over his right brow. And his nose, she realized, was not the straight noble nose of the man she'd fallen in love with last June. His frame had filled out, too. He wore navy slacks and a cream sweater beneath a brown leather bomber jacket.

He still looked dangerous to her peace of mind.

Paige stuffed the teddy bear back into the gift bag and hitched the belt of her robe tighter around her waist. "What are you doing here?" she demanded. "It's practically the middle of the night,"

"Didn't the nurse tell you I was waiting?"

"Yes, but I thought—"

"Thought what? That I'd left?" His gaze lowered to the bag of gifts. "Where else would you expect me to be? My son and I have to spend some time getting acquainted."

Paige turned away, leaning over the bassinet to hide the fear growing in her heart. What if Hollis planned to sue for custody? She pushed the fear away. Hollis had given her his word that he trusted her to do what was best for the baby. Their baby was staring up at them with murky blue eyes. Paige's heart melted with tenderness. "How long do you plan to stay?" she asked mildly.

"That depends on you."

Paige had no idea what that meant. She lifted her gaze to meet his and saw uncertainty in Hollis's gaze. The thought that he felt as vulnerable as she did gave her the courage to speak her mind. "I read your letters."

He raised a gold-tipped brow. "They were addressed to the baby."

"He's too young to read."

"Good thing I held one letter back, then."

A painful lump jammed Paige's throat as he removed an envelope from his pocket. She was terribly afraid that whatever he had to say wouldn't erase the hurt that held her heart hostage. "What does it say?"

"I don't know... I haven't written it yet. It's still

blank.'' His voice lowered to a husky note. ''I made a promise not to try to contact the recipient in any way, and I don't want to break that promise. I'm afraid she won't trust me with something precious if I do.''

Trust. Hot tears pricked her eyes. ''Why don't you tell me what you want to say and I'll tell you if it's worth the risk?''

Hollis took a deep breath and Paige trembled. ''Well, the first lines would go something like, I love you and I'm sorry I didn't tell you who I was before you made love to Matt. I let my ego get in the way. I kept hoping you'd figure out it was me, recognize me. You know, men sort of think they have an original technique that can't be duplicated. It hurt that you didn't know who I was and that you could so easily dismiss your feelings for Hollis and take up with Matt.''

Paige didn't pull any punches. ''Matt had his charms, but he was a liar. I like to think I was subconsciously drawn to the parts of Hollis shining through.''

Hollis's jaw tightened perceptibly. ''What about now? How do you feel about Hollis?''

Paige lowered her eyes to the baby stirring in the bassinet. ''I think he makes beautiful babies, and he'll be a good father.'' She paused.

''And?''

One simple word and she knew with a soul deep certainty he was bracing himself because he was afraid she'd permanently abandon him and was desperately clinging to hopes of his own.

She tilted her chin up and smiled stubbornly.

"And, I'd like to be kissed by Hollis Fenton again before I say anything more."

"That I can oblige you with."

Relief, hope and forgiveness washed through her in a cleansing rush as he by-stepped the bassinet, placing the envelope beside their son's swaddled form and drew her securely into the hardness of his body. Right where she belonged, Paige thought blissfully as his fingers feathered along her neck. His thumb stroked her chin, brushing her lower lip and awakening her body with sweet anticipation. She rose up on tiptoe and met his kiss, hungrily.

She murmured regret when Hollis finally lifted his head. She stared up at him dreamily, savoring the taste of him on her lips. The prospect of a lifetime of loving him filled her with unabashed joy.

"What's the verdict?" Hollis demanded with a very sexy, all-male grin.

Her hand curled around his neck. "I'm willing to give you about twenty seconds to kiss me again or propose, not necessarily in that order. We have a lot of lost time to make up for."

"Good thing I brought the envelope then."

She blinked, uncomprehending as he plucked the envelope from the bassinet and ripped it open. A diamond solitaire ring fell into his palm.

He took her left hand in his strong fingers. His voice rasped with husky emotion. "Paige, this ring is a symbol of my promise to honor and love you in thought, word and deed every day of my life." He kissed the ring he'd placed on her finger, sealing his vow.

She clenched his hand, barely able to choke out a reply through the feelings welling in her. "Not ex-

actly a question, but it'll do. I promise I'll never forget that I love Hollis Fenton, ever again."

"Say it again."

She gazed up into his hazel eyes. "I love you."

The baby stirred and yawned. Paige felt as if her
cup were running over with happiness. "Good, now
that our baby's got a last name, we can settle on a
given name. I was thinking along the lines of Thompson Darby Fenton. Thompson after Brenda because
she brought us together, and Darby, because well,
Matt Darby did have certain charms... What do you
think?"

"I think I haven't kissed you enough if you're still
thinking about Matt Darby."

"You could rectify that situation right now."

And he did until Thompson Darby Fenton let out
a howl and reminded them that he was the center of
their universe.

Author Note

My sincere thanks and gratitude to the following people who've so generously allowed me to pick their brains for Paige and Hollis's journey: Any errors are my own.

Linda and Pat Poitevin; Francois Tremblay; Jackie Oakley and Constable Bob Arbor, Bomb Technician, Ottawa-Carleton Police; Criminologist T. Lorraine Vassalo; Danielle Ferron, Ph.D; Liisa Tuominen, librarian at *The Ottawa Citizen*; *The Globe and Mail* Advertising and Sales Rep, Marilyn Andrews; Journalists Louisa Taylor, Teresa Eckford and Kathryn Young-Davies; Jean Tremblay; Lori Visser-Booth; and Gilles David.

Special thanks to Dr. Stephen W. MacLean.

Amnesia...an unknown danger...
a burning desire.

With

HARLEQUIN®

I N T R I G U E®
you're just

A MEMORY AWAY

from passion, danger...and love!

**Look for all the books in this
exciting miniseries:**

THE BABY SECRET (#546)
by Joyce Sullivan
On sale December 1999

A NIGHT WITHOUT END (#552)
by Susan Kearney
On sale January 2000

FORGOTTEN LULLABY (#556)
by Rita Herron
On sale February 2000

A MEMORY AWAY...—where
remembering the truth becomes
a matter of life, death...and love!

Available at your favorite retail outlet.

If you enjoyed what you just read,
then we've got an offer you can't resist!

Take 2 bestselling love stories FREE!

Plus get a FREE surprise gift!

Coming in January 2000
Classics for two of your favorite series.

 SECRET VOWS by **REBECCA YORK** & **KELSEY ROBERTS**

From the best of Rebecca York's

43 Light St.

Till Death Us Do Part

Marissa Devereaux discovered that paradise wasn't all it was cracked up to be when she was abducted by extremists on the Caribbean island of Costa Verde.... But things only got worse when Jed Prentiss showed up, claiming to be her fiancé.

From the best of Kelsey Roberts's

THE ROSE TATTOO

Unlawfully Wedded

J.D. was used to getting what he wanted from people, and he swore he'd use that skill to hunt down Tory's father's killer. But J.D. wanted much more than gratitude from his sassy blond bride—and he wasn't going to clue her in. She'd find out soon enough...if she survived to hear about it.

Available January 2000 at your favorite retail outlet.

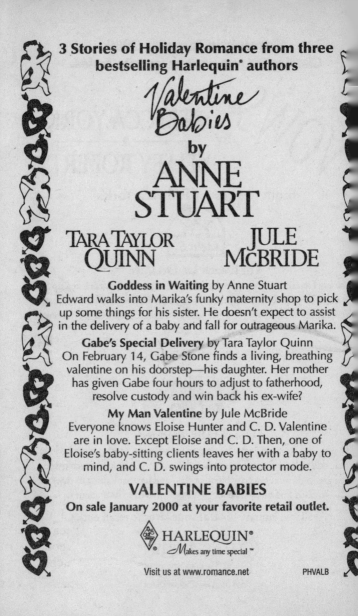

COMING NEXT MONTH

Harlequin Intrigue has a *new* cover look—
watch for us at your favorite retail outlet!

#549 THE LITTLEST WITNESS by Amanda Stevens
Gallagher Justice

The assumed identities of Thea Lockhart and her four-year-old daughter were jeopardized when the child witnessed a murder. Forced to cooperate with Detective John Gallagher, Thea knew working closely with him could prove dangerous to their secret—and her heart. Could Thea hide her past from the man she desperately wanted in her future?

#550 CAPTURED BY A SHEIKH by Jacqueline Diamond

Holly Rivers had been swept away from the altar by a sheikh in flowing robes who claimed her nephew was his son. Held captive by Sharif Al-Khalil, Holly found the man a fierce protector of his family, a formidable enemy and a fantastic lover. Sharif and his son appeared to be the targets of the threats, but when the madman set his sights on Holly, he crossed the line.

#551 MY BABY, MY LOVE by Dani Sinclair

Widowed, pregnant and the only living eyewitness to a robbery, Sydney Edwards needed Noah Inglewood's protection—and the thieves needed something from Sydney. But Noah was determined to keep the woman and the child she carried safe from harm. His instincts warned that the robbers' vendetta was personal—but so was his involvement with Sydney.

#552 A NIGHT WITHOUT END by Susan Kearney
A Memory Away...

Carlie Myers wasn't really Sean McCabe's wife—she was the key to his partner's murder. Until Carlie regained her memory, Sean wanted her nearby, but he didn't expect the sizzling attraction that seared between them to assist his charade. Being in close proximity with Carlie made Sean forget the arrangement was temporary, and that was dangerous while the real killer still lurked....

Visit us at www.romance.net

Who was the father of her baby?

Waking up with a raging headache and nausea, Paige Roberts couldn't remember the past six weeks of her life! And when her symptoms turned out to be much more than the flu, Paige was stunned. A baby! But who was the father? And why was she so attracted to her charming but mysterious new neighbor?

Matt Darby couldn't believe Paige didn't remember their steamy nights together—or the explosion that nearly killed them both. Somehow Matt had to jar Paige's shattered memories without revealing his true identity. But when he learned he was going to be a father, Matt's desperation grew. Because a killer was on the hunt, after him—and after Paige, the only witness to a horrible crime....

A MEMORY AWAY...
from passion, danger— and love!

HARLEQUIN®
Makes any time special ™

ISBN 0-373-22546-6

22546

0 65373 00399 7